"A work of sheer exhilaration. . . . As exciting and entertaining a story as you're likely to read."
                                        —*Chicago Sun-Times*

"Fun. . . . Reilly keep[s] the action coming."
                                        —*Kirkus Reviews*

"Ancient history, heart-stopping booby traps, and wild adventure . . . a perfect book to jump-start your vacation beach reading."   —*Library Journal*

"A nonstop roller-coaster ride."   —*Publishers Weekly*

ICE STATION

"Some of the wildest and most sustained battles in an action thriller in a long time. . . . Nonstop action, lots of explosions—and a little bit of conspiracy."
                                        —*Chicago Tribune*

"Nonstop, brain-freezing action from page 1."
                                        —*The Tulsa World*

TEMPLE

"Reilly's book has adrenaline in super-sized quantities."
                                        —*Orlando Sentinel*

"The action is relentless."   —*Charleston Post and Courier*

AREA 7

"Reilly's . . . most suspenseful blow-'em-up. The jet-boat chase through the blind chasms of Arizona's Lake Powell puts the Bond books to shame."
                                        —*Kirkus Reviews* (starred review)

ALSO BY MATTHEW REILLY

MATTHEW REILLY

HELL ISLAND

POCKET BOOKS

NEW YORK   LONDON   TORONTO   SYDNEY

Pocket Books
A Division of Simon & Schuster, Inc.
1230 Avenue of the Americas
New York, NY 10020

This book is a work of fiction. Names, characters, places, and incidents either are products of the author's imagination or are used fictitiously. Any resemblance to actual events or locales or persons, living or dead, is entirely coincidental.

Originally published in Australia by Books Alive,
an Australian Government initiative developed through the
Australia Council for the Arts.

First Pocket Books paperback edition October 2010

POCKET and colophon are registered trademarks of Simon & Schuster, Inc.

For information about special discounts for bulk purchases, please contact Simon & Schuster Special Sales at 1-866-506-1949 or business@simonandschuster.com.

The Simon & Schuster Speakers Bureau can bring authors to your live event. For more information or to book an event contact the Simon & Schuster Speakers Bureau at 1-866-248-3049 or visit our website at www.simonspeakers.com.

All non-map illustrations by Tyler Jacobson

Manufactured in the United States of America

10   9   8   7   6   5

ISBN 978-1-4391-9133-0

INTRODUCTION

It may surprise some people, but of all the books I've written, *Hell Island* has been the most rewarding. Allow me to explain.

As many readers will notice immediately, it is a lot shorter than my other novels. But there's a reason for this.

Hell Island was originally written for an Australian Government initiative called Books Alive, the objective of which was to get Australians into bookstores and reading more. I was approached to write a short novel, no longer than 110 pages, that would be given away to Australians for free for a month. I thought this was a fantastic idea and jumped at the chance.

I wrote *Hell Island*.

More than that, I set out to write 110 pages of the most kick-butt, over-the-top, blindingly fast action I could. It's not often you get a chance to show your stuff to the general population *for free,* so I seized the opportunity with both hands.

Anyway, the initiative was a roaring success, with over a quarter of a million copies of *Hell Island* given away. (While Australian readers received the book for free, within days of its release, copies of the book found their way onto eBay, where Aussies were selling them to my American fans for fifty bucks!)

In the time since *Hell Island*'s original release, though, something strange has happened.

When I do book signings, I often ask my readers, "So, which was the first book of mine that you read?" The most common replies used to be *Ice Station* or *Contest*.

But these days, it's *Hell Island*.

And I think the reason is: It's short.

My books have a huge success rate with getting reluctant readers (especially teenage boys) into reading. And when you offer a reluctant reader a short novel, they think: *Okay, it's only 110 pages, I can manage that.*

And since *Hell Island* is a non-stop rampage of all-out action from start to finish—with special forces soldiers going up against an unstoppable and pitiless enemy—the reluctant reader gets into it, enjoys it, and goes on to try a full-length novel. And thus a new reader is created. This is why *Hell Island* has been so rewarding for me.

Hell Island was an absolute blast to write and the response to it has exceeded my wildest expectations—so much so, in fact, that I've actually written another short novel recently.

But that's enough from me. Now, on with the show . . .

MR
Sydney, Australia

HELL ISLAND

PROLOGUE

THE LAST MAN STANDING

TERRIFIED, WOUNDED and now out of ammo, Lieutenant Rick "Razor" Haynes staggered down the tight passageway, blood pouring from a gunshot wound to his left thigh, scratch-marks crisscrossing his face.

He panted as he moved, gasping for breath. He was the last one left, the last member of his entire Marine force still alive.

He could hear them behind him.

Grunting, growling.

Stalking him, hunting him down.

They *knew* they had him—knew he was out of ammunition, out of contact with base, and out of comrades-in-arms.

The passageway through which he was fleeing was long and straight, barely wide enough for his shoulders. It had gray steel walls studded with rivets—the kind you find on a military vessel, a warship.

Wincing in agony, Haynes arrived at a bulkhead doorway and fell clumsily through it, landing in a stateroom. He reached up and pulled the heavy steel door shut behind him.

The door closed and he spun the flywheel.

A second later, the great steel door shuddered violently, pounded from the other side.

His face covered in sweat, Haynes breathed deeply, glad for the brief reprieve.

He'd seen what they had done to his teammates, and been horrified.

No soldier deserved to die that way, or to have his body desecrated in such a manner. It was beyond ruthless what they'd done to his men.

That said, the way they had systematically overcome his force of six hundred United States Marines had been tactically brilliant.

At one point during his escape from the hangar deck, Haynes figured he'd end his own life before they caught him. Now, without any bullets, he couldn't even do that.

A grunt disturbed him.

It had come from nearby. From the darkness on the other side of the stateroom.

Haynes snapped to look up—

—just as a shape came rushing out of the darkness, a dark hairy shape, man-sized, screaming a fierce high-pitched shriek, like the cry of a deranged chimpanzee.

Only this was no chimpanzee.

It slammed into Haynes, ramming him back against the door. His head hit the steel door hard, the blow stunning him but not knocking him out.

And as he slumped to the floor and saw the creature draw a glistening long-bladed K-Bar knife from its sheath, Haynes wished it *had* knocked him unconscious, because then he wouldn't have to witness what it did to him next . . .

The death-scream of Razor Haynes echoed out from the aircraft carrier.

It would not be heard by a single friendly soul.

For this carrier was a long way from anywhere, docked at an old World War II refueling station in the middle of the Pacific, a station attached to a small island that had curiously ceased to appear on maps after the Americans had taken it by force from the Japanese in 1943.

Once known as Grant Island, it was a thousand kilometers south of the Bering Strait and five hundred from its nearest island neighbor. In the war it had seen fierce fighting as the Americans had wrested it—and its highly-prized airfield—from a suicidal Japanese garrison.

Because of the ferocity of the fighting and the heavy losses incurred there, Grant Island was given another name by the U.S. Marines who'd fought there.

They called it Hell Island.

FIRST ASSAULT

HELL ISLAND

1500 HOURS

1 AUGUST

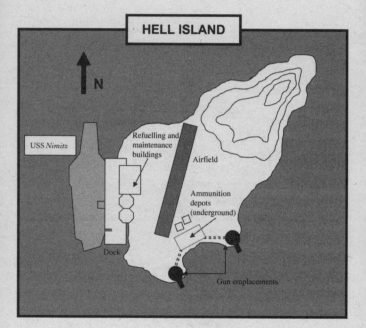

The vicious-looking aircraft shot across the sky at near supersonic speed.

It was a modified Hercules cargo plane, known as an MC-130 "Combat Talon," the delivery vehicle of choice for U.S. Special Forces units.

This Combat Talon stayed high, very high, it was as if it was trying to avoid being seen by radar systems down at sea level. This was unusual, because there was nothing down there —according to the maps, the nearest land in this part of the Pacific was an atoll 500 klicks to the east.

Then the rear loading ramp of the Combat Talon rumbled open and several dozen tiny figures issued out from it in rapid sequence, spreading out into the sky behind the soaring plane.

The forty-strong flock of paratroopers plummeted to earth, men in high-altitude jumpsuits—full-face breathing masks; streamlined black bodysuits. They angled their bodies downward as they fell, so that they

flew head-first, their masks pointed into the onrushing wind, becoming human spears, freefalling with serious intent.

It was a classic HALO drop—high-altitude, low-opening. You jumped from 37,000 feet, fell fast and hard, and then stopped dangerously close to the ground, right at your drop zone.

Curiously, however, the forty elite troops falling to earth today fell in identifiable subgroups, ten men to a group, as if they were trying to remain somehow separate.

Indeed, they were separate teams.

Crack teams. The best of the best from every corner of the U.S. armed forces.

One unit from the 82nd Airborne Division.

One SEAL team.

One Delta team, ever aloof and secretive.

And last of all, one team of Force Reconnaissance Marines.

They shot into the cloud layer—a dense band of dark thunderclouds—freefell through the haze.

Then after nearly a full minute of flying, they burst out of the clouds and emerged in the midst of a full-scale five-alarm ocean storm: rain lashed their facemasks; dark clouds hung low over the heaving ocean; giant waves rolled and crashed.

And through the rain, their target came into view,

a tiny island far below them, an island that did not appear on maps anymore, an island with an aircraft carrier parked alongside it.

Hell.

Leading the Marine team was Captain Shane M. Schofield, call-sign "Scarecrow."

Behind his HALO mask, Schofield had a rugged creased face, black hair and blue eyes. Slicing down across those eyes, however, were a pair of hideous vertical scars, one for each eye, wounds from a mission-gone-wrong and the source of his operational nickname. Once on the ground, he'd hide those eyes behind a pair of reflective wraparound anti-flash glasses.

Quiet, intense and when necessary deadly, Schofield had a unique reputation in the Marine Corps. He'd been involved in several missions that remained classified—but the Marine Corps (like any group of human beings) is filled with gossip and rumor. Someone always knew someone who was there, or who saw the medical report, or who cleaned up the aftermath.

The rumors about Schofield were many and varied, and sometimes simply too outrageous to be true.

One: he had been involved in a gigantic multiforce battle in Antarctica, a battle which, it was said, involved a bloody and brutal confrontation with two of America's allies, France and Britain.

Two: he'd saved the President during an attempted

military coup at a remote USAF base. It was said that during that misadventure, the Scarecrow—a former pilot—had flown an experimental space shuttle into low earth orbit, engaged an enemy shuttle, destroyed it, and then come *back* to earth to rescue the President.

Of course none of this could possibly be verified, and so it remained the stuff of legend; legends, however, that Schofield's new unit were acutely aware of.

That said, there was one thing about Shane Schofield that they knew to be true: this was his first mission back after a long layover, four months of stress leave, in fact. On this occasion someone really *had* seen the medical report, and now all of his men on this mission knew about it.

They also knew the cause of his stress leave.

During his last mission out, Schofield had been taken to the very edge of his psychological endurance. Loved ones close to him had been captured . . . and executed. It was even said in hushed whispers that at one point on that mission he had tried to take his own life.

Which was why the other members of his team today were slightly less-than-confident in their leader.

Was he up to this mission? Was he a time-bomb waiting to explode? Was he a basketcase who would lose it at the first sign of trouble?

They were about to find out.

AS HE shot downward through the sky, Schofield recalled their mission briefing earlier that day.

Their target was Hell Island.

Actually, that wasn't quite true.

Their target was the aging supercarrier parked at Hell Island, the USS *Nimitz,* CVN-68.

The problem: soon after it had arrived at the isolated island to pick up some special cargo, a devastating tsunami had struck from the north and all contact with the *Nimitz* had been lost.

The oldest of America's twelve *Nimitz*-class carriers, the *Nimitz* had been heading home for decommissioning, with only a skeleton crew of 500 aboard—down from its regular 6,000. Likewise, its Carrier Battle Group, the cluster of destroyers, subs, supply ships and frigates that normally accompanied it around the globe, had been trimmed to just two cruisers.

Contact with the two escort boats and the island's communications center had also been lost.

Unfortunately, the unexpected tidal wave wasn't the only hostile entity in play here: a North Korean nu-

clear submarine had been spotted a day earlier coming out of the Bering Sea. Its whereabouts were currently unknown, its presence in this area suspicious.

And so a mystery.

Equally suspicious to Schofield, however, was the presence of the other special operations units on this mission: the 82nd, the SEALs and Delta.

This was exceedingly odd. You never mixed and matched special ops units. They all had different specialties, different approaches to mission situations, and could easily trip over each other. In short, it just wasn't done.

You added all that up, Schofield thought, and this smelled suspiciously like an exercise.

Except for one thing.

They were all carrying live ammunition.

Hurtling toward the world, freefalling at terminal velocity, bursting out of the cloudband . . .

. . . to behold the Pacific Ocean stretching away in every direction, the only imperfection in its surface: the small dot of land that was Hell Island.

A gigantic rectangular gray object lay at its western end, the *Nimitz*. Not far from the carrier, the island featured some big gun emplacements facing south and east, while at the northeastern tip there was a hill that looked like a mini-volcano.

A voice came through Schofield's earpiece. *"All team leaders, this is Delta Six. We're going for the eastern end of the island and we'll work our way back to the boat. Your DZ is the flight deck: Airborne, the bow; SEALs, aft; Marines, mid-section."*

Just like we were told in the briefing, Schofield thought.

This was typical of Delta. They were born show-ponies. Great soldiers, sure, but glory-seekers all. No matter who they were working with—even today, alongside three of the best special forces units in the world—they always assumed they were in charge.

"Roger that, Delta leader," came the SEAL leader's voice.

"Copy, Delta Six," came the Airborne response.

Schofield didn't reply.

The Delta leader said, *"Marine Six? Scarecrow? You copy?"*

Schofield sighed. "I was at the mission briefing, too, Delta Six. And last I noticed, I don't have any short-term memory problems. I know the mission plan."

"Cut the attitude, Scarecrow," the Delta leader said. His name was Hugh Gordon, so naturally his call-sign was "Flash." *"We're all on the same team here."*

"What? *Your* team?" Schofield said. "How about this: how about you don't break radio silence until you've got something important to say. Scarecrow, out."

It was more important than that. Even a frequency-hopping encrypted radio signal could be caught these days, so if you transmitted, you had to assume someone was listening.

Worse, the new French-made Signet-5 radio-wave decoder—sold by the French to Russia, Iran, North Korea, Syria and other fine upstanding global citizens—was specifically designed to seek out *and locate* the American AN/PRC-119 tactical radio when it was broadcasting, the very radio their four teams were using today. No one had yet thought to ask the French why they had built a locater whose only use was to pinpoint American tactical radios.

Schofield switched to his team's private channel. "Marines. Switch off your tac radios. Listening mode only. Go to short-wave UHF if you want to talk to me."

A few of his Marines hesitated before obeying, but obey they did. They flicked off their radios.

The four clusters of parachutists plummeted through the storm toward the world, zeroing in on the *Nimitz,* until a thousand feet above it, they yanked on their ripcords and their chutes opened.

Their superfast falls were abruptly arrested and they now floated in toward the carrier. The Delta team landed on the island itself, while the other three teams touched down lightly and gracefully on the flight deck of the supercarrier right in their assigned positions—fore, mid and aft—guns up.

They had just arrived in Hell.

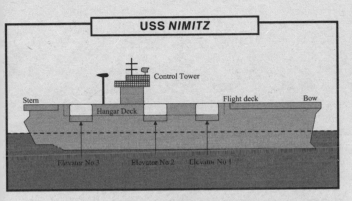

USS NIMITZ

Control Tower

Stern · Hangar Deck · Flight deck · Bow

Elevator No 3 · Elevator No 2 · Elevator No 1

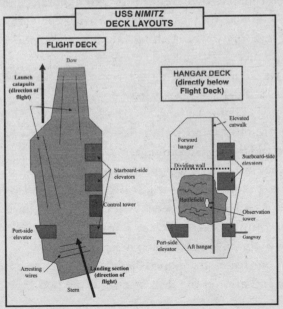

USS NIMITZ DECK LAYOUTS

FLIGHT DECK

Bow

Launch catapults (direction of flight)

Starboard-side elevators

Control tower

Port-side elevator

Arresting wires

Landing section (direction of flight)

Stern

HANGAR DECK (directly below Flight Deck)

Elevated catwalk

Forward hangar

Dividing wall

Starboard-side elevators

Battlefield

Observation tower

Port-side elevator

Aft hangar

Gangway

RAIN HAMMERED down on the flight deck.

Schofield's team landed one after the other, unclipping their chutes before the great mushroom-shaped canopies had even hit the ground. The chutes were whipped away by the wind, leaving the ten Marines standing in the slashing rain on the flight deck, holding their MP-7s pointed outwards.

One after the other, they ripped off their face-masks, scanned the deck warily.

Schofield shucked his facemask and donned his signature silver wraparound glasses, masking his eyes. He beheld the deck around them.

The entire flight deck was deserted.

Except for the other teams that had just landed on it, not a soul could be seen. A few planes sat parked on the runways, some Tomcats and Hornets, and one chunky CH-53 Super Stallion helicopter.

There were star-shaped blood splatters on all of them, and also on the deck itself. But no bodies. Not one.

"Mother," Schofield said to his number two, "what do you think?"

"What do I think?" the bulky female Marine to his right replied. "I think this is seriously fucked up. I was planning on spending this weekend watching David Hasselhoff DVDs. No one takes me away from the Hoff."

Gena Newman was her real name, Gunnery Sergeant was her rank, but "Mother" was her call-sign and it didn't relate to any overtly maternal traits. It was short for a slightly longer word starting with "Mother."

At six-feet-two, 200 pounds, and with a fully-shaven head, Mother cut a mean figure. Tough, no-nonsense and fiercely loyal, she had accompanied Schofield on many missions, including the bad ones. She was also arguably the best Gunny in the Corps—once she had even been offered her pick of assignments *outside* Schofield's command. She'd looked the Commandant of the Marine Corps in the eye and said, "I'm staying with the Scarecrow, sir."

Mother gazed at the blood splatters on a nearby plane. "No, this was way suspect from the start. I mean, why are we here with D-boys, Airbornes and slithery SEALs? I'd rather just work with swordsmen."

Swordsman was her word for a Marine: a reference to the swords they wore with their full-dress uniforms.

"Marines," Schofield called, "the tower. Let's move."

Since they'd been assigned the mid-section of the supercarrier, Schofield's Marines had the task of investigating the carrier's six-story-high command tower,

known as "the Island." But since this mission also involved a real island, it was being referred to today as "the tower."

They moved quickly through the rain, crossed the wide flight deck, arrived at the base of the tower—to find the main door there covered in blood and about a million bullet holes. It hung askew, its hinges blasted.

Looking up, Schofield saw that every single antenna and radar array atop the command tower had been broken or destroyed. The main antenna mast was broken in the middle and now lay tilted over.

"What in God's name happened here?" one of Schofield's Marines asked softly. He was a big guy, broad-shouldered, with a super solid footballer's neck. His name: Corporal Harold "Hulk" Hogan.

"Not a tsunami, that's for sure," Sergeant Paulo "Pancho" Sanchez said. Older and more senior than Hulk, he was a sly sarcastic type. "Tsunamis don't shoot you in the head."

The voice of the SEAL leader came through their earpieces: *"All units, this is Gator, Starboard Elevator Three has been disabled. We're taking the stairs, heading for the main hangar bay below the flight deck."*

"This is Condor," the Airborne leader called in. *"I got evidence of a firefight in the SAM launcher bay up at the bow. Lot of blood, but not a single body . . ."*

"Delta Six here. We're on the island proper. No sign of anything yet . . ."

Schofield didn't send out any report.

"Sir," Sanchez said to him. "You gonna call in?"

"No."

Sanchez exchanged a quick look with the Marine next to him, a tall guy named Bigfoot. Sanchez was one of the men who'd been dubious about Schofield's mental state and his ability to lead this mission.

"Not even to tell the others where we are?"

"No."

"But what about—"

"Sergeant," Schofield said sharply, "did you ask your previous commander to explain everything to you?"

"No, sir."

"So don't start doing it now. Focus on the mission at hand."

Sanchez bit his lip and nodded. "Yes, sir."

"Now, if no one else has anything to say, let's take this tower. Move."

Hurdling the twisted steel door, they charged into the darkness of the supercarrier's command tower.

UP A series of tight ladders that formed the spine of the command tower, moving quickly. Blood on the rungs.

Still no bodies.

Schofield's team came to the bridge, the middle of three glass-enclosed lookout levels on the tower.

They were granted a superb view of the flight deck outside . . . albeit through cracked and smashed wrap-around windows.

Nearly every window overlooking the flight deck had been destroyed. Blood dripped off what glass remained. Thousands of spent rounds littered the floor. Also, a few guns lay about: mainly M-16s, plus a few M-4 Colt Commandos, the short-barreled version of the M-16 used by special forces teams worldwide.

Mother led a sub-team upstairs, to the uppermost bridge: the flight control bridge. She returned a few minutes later.

"Same deal," she reported. "Bucketloads of blood, no bodies. All windows smashed, and an armory's worth of spent ammo left on the floor. A hell of a fire-fight took place here, Scarecrow."

"A firefight that was cleaned up afterward," Schofield said.

Just then, something caught his eye: one of the abandoned rifles on the floor, one of the M-4s.

He picked it up, examined it.

From a distance it looked like a regular M-4, but it wasn't. It had been modified slightly.

The gun's trigger-guard was different: it had been elongated, as if to accommodate a *longer* index finger that wrapped itself around the gun's trigger.

"What the hell is that?" Hulk said, seeing it. "Some kind of super gun?"

"Scarecrow," Mother said, coming over. "Most of these blood splatters are the result of bullet impacts. But some aren't. They're . . . well . . . thicker. More like arterial flow. As if some of the dead had entire *limbs* cut off."

Schofield's earpiece squawked.

"All units, this is Gator. My SEAL team has just arrived at the main hangar deck and holy shit, people, have we got something to show you. We aren't the first force to have got here. And the guys before us didn't fare well at all. I have a visual on at least two hundred pairs of hands all stacked up in a neat pile down here."

Sanchez whispered, "Did he just say—?"

Gator anticipated this. *"Yes, you heard me right. Hands. Human hands. Cut off and stacked in a great big heap. What in God's name have we walked into here?"*

WHILE THE rest of their team listened in horror to Gator's gruesome report, Schofield and Mother strode into the command center, the inner section of the bridge. It too was largely wrecked, but not totally.

"Mother, do a power-grid check, all grids, all levels, even externals. I'm gonna look for ATOs."

Mother sat down at an undamaged console while Schofield went to the Captain's desk and attached some C-2 low-expansion plastic explosive to the commanding officer's safe.

A muffled boom later and he had the *Nimitz's* last fourteen ATOs—Air Tasking Orders, the ship's daily orders received from Pacific Command at Pearl Harbor.

It was mainly routine stuff as the *Nimitz* hopscotched her way back from the Indian Ocean to Hawaii, dropping in at Singapore and the Philippines on the way . . .

Until ten days ago . . .

. . . when the *Nimitz* was ordered to divert to the Japanese island of Okinawa and pick up three companies of U.S. Marines there, a force of about 600 men.

She was to ferry the Marines—not crack Recon

troops, but rather just regular men—across the northern Pacific and drop them off at a set of coordinates that Schofield knew to be Hell Island.

After unloading the Marines, the ship was then instructed to:

PICK UP DARPA SCIENCE TEAM FROM LOCATION:

KNOX, MALCOLM C.	RYAN, HARPER R.
PENNEBAKER, ZACHARY B.	HOGAN, SHANE M.
JOHNSON, SIMON W.	LIEBMANN, BEN C.
HENDRICKS, JAMES F.	

PERSONNEL ARE ALL SECURITY-CLEARED TO "TOP SECRET." THEY WILL HAVE CARGO WHICH IS NOT TO BE SEEN BY CREW OF *NIMITZ*.

So. The *Nimitz* had been sent here to drop off a sizeable force of Marines and also pick up some scientists who had been at work here.

Again, it bore all the hallmarks of an exercise—Marines being unloaded on a secret island where DARPA scientists had been at work.

DARPA was the Defense Advanced Research Projects Agency, the genius-level scientists who made high-tech weaponry for the U.S. military. After inventing the Internet and stealth technology, rumor had it that DARPA had recently been at work on ultra-high-tensile, low-weight body armor and, notoriously, a fourth-generation thermonuclear weapon called a *Supernova,* the most powerful nuke ever devised.

"Scarecrow," Mother said from her console. "I got a power drain in grid 14.2, the starboard-side router, going to an external destination, location unknown. Something on the island is draining power from the *Nimitz*'s reactor. Beyond that, all other electrical systems on the boat have been shut down: lights, air-conditioning, everything."

Schofield thought about that.

"And another thing," Mother said. "I fired up the ship's internal spectrum analyzer. I'm picking up a weird radio signal being transmitted inside the *Nimitz*."

"Why's it weird?"

"Because it's not a voice signal. It sounds, well, like a digital signal, a binary beep sequence. Fact, sounds like my old dial-up modem."

Schofield frowned. A power drain going off the ship. Digital radio signals inside the ship. A secret DARPA presence. And a gruesome stack of severed hands down in the hangar deck.

This didn't make sense at all.

"Mother," he said, "you got a portable AXS on you?" An AXS was an AXS-9 radio spectrum analyzer, a portable unit that picked up radio transmissions, a bug detector.

"Sure have."

"Jamming capabilities?"

"Multi-channel or single channel," she said.

"Good," Schofield said. "Tune it in to those beeps. Stay on them. And just be ready to jam them."

Gator's voice continued to come over his earpiece. The SEAL leader was describing the scene in the hangar bay:

"*. . . looks like the entire hangar has been configured for an exercise of some sort. It's like an indoor battlefield. I got artificial trenches, some low terrain, even a field tower set up inside the hangar. Moving toward the nearest trench now—hey, what was that. . . ? Holy—*"

Gunfire rang out. Sustained automatic gunfire.

Both from the SEALs and from an unknown enemy force. The SEALs' silenced MP-5SNs made a chilling *slit-slit-slit-slit-slit-slit* when they fired. Their enemies' guns made a different noise altogether, the distinct puncture-like clatter of M-4 Colt Commando assault rifles.

The SEALs starting shouting to each other:

"*—they're coming out of the nearest trench—*"

"*—what the* fuck *is that . . .*"

"*—it looks like a Goddamn go—*"

Sprack! The speaker never finished his sentence. The sound of a bullet slamming into his skull echoed through his radio-mike.

Then Gator's voice: "*Fire! Open fire! Mow 'em down!*"

In response to the order, the level of SEAL gunfire intensified. But the SEALs' voices became more desperate.

"*—Jesus, they just keep coming! There are too many of them!*"

"—*Get back to the stairs! Get back to the*—"

"—*Shit! There are more back there! They're cutting us off! They've got us surrounded!*"

A pained scream.

"—*Gator's down! Oh, fuck, ah*—"

The speaker's voice was abruptly cut off by a guttural grunting sound that all but *ate* his radio-mike. The man screamed, a terrified shriek that was muffled by rough scuffling noises over his mike. He panted desperately as if struggling with some great beast. Indeed it sounded as if some kind of frenzied creature had barreled into him full-tilt *and started eating his face.*

Then *blam!* a gunshot boomed and there were no more screams. Schofield couldn't tell if it was the man who had fired or the thing that had attacked him.

And suddenly it was over.

Silence on the airwaves.

In the bridge of the supercarrier, the members of Schofield's team swapped glances.

Sanchez reached for the radio—only for Schofield to swat his hand away.

"I said no signals."

Sanchez scowled, but obeyed.

One of the other teams, however, came over the line: "*SEAL team, this is Condor. What's going on? Come in!*"

Schofield waited for a reply.

None came.

But then after thirty seconds or so, another rough scuffling sound could be heard, someone—or some-thing—grabbing one of the SEAL team's radio-mikes.

Then a terrifying sound shot through the radio.

A horrific animal roar.

SEAL TEAM, *I repeat! This is Condor! Come in!*" the Airborne commander kept saying over the radio.

"Scarecrow!" Mother exclaimed. "I got something here . . ."

"What?" Schofield hurried over to her console.

"Those binary beeps just went off the charts. It's like a thousand fax machines all dialed up at once. There was a jump thirty seconds ago as well, just after Condor called the SEALs the first time."

"Shit . . ." Schofield said. "Quickly, Mother. Find the ship's dry-dock security systems. Initiate the motion sensors."

Every American warship had standard security features for use when they were in dry-dock. One was an infrared motion sensor array positioned throughout the ship's main corridors—to detect intruders who might enter the boat when it was deserted. The USS *Nimitz* possessed just such a system.

"Got it," Mother said.

"Initialize," Schofield said.

A wire-frame image of the *Nimitz* appeared on a

big freestanding glass screen in the center of the control room, a cross-section shown from the right-hand side.

"Holy shit . . ." Hulk said, seeing the screen.

"Mama mia . . ." Sanchez breathed.

A veritable *river* of red dots was flowing out from the main hangar bay, heading toward the bow of the carrier . . . where a far smaller cluster of ten dots stood stationary: Condor's Airborne team.

Each dot represented an individual moving past the infrared sensors. There were perhaps 400 dots on the screen right now. And they were moving at incredible speed, practically leap-frogging each other in their frenzy to get forward.

For Schofield, things were starting to make sense.

The binary beeps were the encrypted digital communications of his enemy, spiking whenever they radioed each other. He also now knew for sure that they had Signet-5 radio tracers. Damn.

"SEAL team! Come in!" Condor said again over the airwaves.

"Another spike in the digital chatter," Mother reported.

The dots on the glass screen picked up their pace.

"Christ. He's got to get off the air," Schofield said. "He's bringing them right to him."

"We have to tell him, warn him . . ." Sanchez said.

"How?" Mother demanded. "If we call him on our radios, we'll only be giving away our own position."

"We can't just leave him there, with all those things on the way!"

"Wanna bet?" Mother said.

"The Airborne guys know their job," Schofield interrupted. "As do we. And our job is not to babysit them. We have to trust they know what they're doing. We also have our own mission: to find out what's been happening here and to end it. Which is why we're going down to the main hangar right now."

Schofield's team hustled out of the bridge, sliding down the drop-ladders.

Last to leave was Sanchez, covering the rear.

With a final glare at Schofield, he pulled out his radio, selected the Airborne team's private channel, and started talking.

Then he took off after the others.

Descending through the tower, the Marines came level with the flight deck, but instead of going outside, they kept climbing down, heading belowdecks.

Through some tight passageways, lighting the way with their helmet- and barrel-mounted flashlights.

Blood smears lined the walls.

All was dark and grim.

But still no bodies, no nothing.

Then over the main radio network came the sound

of gunfire: Condor's Airborne team had engaged the enemy.

Desperate shouts, screams, sustained fire. Men dying, one by one, just as had happened to the SEAL team.

Listening in, Mother stopped briefly at a security checkpoint—a small computer console sunk into the corridor's wall. These consoles were linked to the *Nimitz*'s security system and on them she could bring up the digital cross-section of the ship, showing where the motion sensors had been triggered.

Right now—to the sound of the Airborne team's desperate shouts—she could see the large swarm of red dots at the right-hand end of the image overwhelming the Airborne team.

In the center of the digital *Nimitz* was her own team, heading for the hangar.

But then there was a sudden change in the image.

A subset of the 400-strong swarm of dots—a subgroup of perhaps forty dots—abruptly broke away from the main group at the bow and started heading *back* toward the hangar.

"Scarecrow . . ." Mother called, "I got hostiles coming back from the bow. Coming back toward us."

"How many?" *And how did they know . . . ?*

"Thirty, maybe forty."

"We can handle forty of anything. Come on."

They continued running as the final transmission from the Airborne team came in. Condor shouting, *"Jesus, there are just too ma— Ahhh!"*

Static.

Then nothing.

The Marine team kept moving.

At the rear in the team, Sanchez came alongside the youngest member of Schofield's unit, a 21-year-old corporal named Sean Miller. Fresh-faced, fit and a science-fiction movie nut, his call-sign was Astro.

"Yo, Astro, you digging this?"

Astro ignored him, just kept peering left and right as he moved.

Sanchez persisted. "I'm telling you, kid, the skip's gone Section Eight. Lost it."

Astro turned briefly. "Hey. Pancho. Until *you* go undefeated at R7, I'll follow the Cap'n."

R7 stood for *Relampago Rojo-7,* the special forces exercises that had been run in conjunction with the huge all-forces Joint Task Force Exercise in Florida in 2004.

Sanchez said, "Hey, hey, hey. The Scarecrow wasn't the only guy to go undefeated at R7. The Buck also did."

The Buck was Captain William Broyles, "the Buccaneer," a brilliant warrior and the former leader of what was acknowledged to be the best Marine Force Reconnaissance Unit, Unit 1.

Sanchez went on: "Fact is, the Buck won the overall exercise on points, because he beat the other teams faster than the Scarecrow did. Shit, the only reason the Scarecrow got a draw with the Buck was because he evaded the Buck's team till the entire exercise timed out."

"A draw's a draw," Astro shrugged. "And, er, didn't you used to be in the Buck's unit?"

"Damn straight," Sanchez said. "So was Biggie. But they disbanded Unit 1 a few months ago and we've been shuffled from team to team ever since, ending up with you guys for this catastrophe."

"So you're biased."

"So I'm cautious. And you should be, too, 'cause we might just be working under a boss who's not firing on all cylinders."

"I'll take that under advisement. Now shut up, we're here."

Sanchez looked forward, and paused.

They'd arrived at the main hangar deck.

SHANE SCHOFIELD stepped out onto a catwalk suspended from the ceiling of the main hangar deck of the USS *Nimitz*. It was an ultra-long catwalk that ran for the entire length of the hangar in a north-south direction, hanging a hundred feet above the floor.

An indoor space the size of two football fields lay beneath him, stretching away to the left and right. Normally it would have been filled with assorted jets, planes, Humvees and trucks.

But not today.

Today it was very, very different.

Schofield recalled Gator's description of the hangar deck:

"It's like an indoor battlefield. I got artificial trenches, some low terrain, even a field tower set up inside the hangar."

It was true.

The hangar deck had indeed been converted into a mock battlefield.

However it had been done, it had been a gargantuan effort, involving the transplanting of several million tons of earth. The end result: something that

looked like the Somme in World War I—a great muddy field, featuring four parallel trenches, low undulating hills and one high steel-legged tower that rose sixty feet off the ground right in the center of the enormous space.

The regular residents of the hangar lay parked at the stern end of the hangar: two F-14 Tomcats, an Osprey, some of the other leftover planes of the *Nimitz,* and some trucks.

The tower was connected to Schofield's ceiling catwalk via a thin steeply-slanted gangway-bridge also suspended from the ceiling.

Schofield said, "Astro and Bigfoot, cover the catwalk to the north of this bridge. Sanchez and Hulk, you got the south side. Call me on the UHF the second you see anything."

Accompanied by the rest of his team, Schofield then crossed the gangway-bridge, came to the observation platform at the top of the field tower.

Broken computers and torn printouts littered the platform. Blood was everywhere.

"What the hell was this place?" Hulk asked.

"An observation post. From here, the big kahunas watched the exercises down on the hangar floor," Mother said.

"But the exercises, it seems, went seriously wrong . . ." Schofield said, examining a printout. Like most of the other material lying around, it was headed:

PROJECT STORMTROOPER

SECURITY CLASSIFICATION:

TOP SECRET-2X

DARPA/U.S. ARMY

"Stormtrooper . . ." he read aloud.

Movement out of the corner of his eye.

Schofield spun—just as an attacker came bursting out of a cabinet at the back of the observation platform.

Six guns swirled as one, locking onto the attacker. But not a single one fired—since the "attacker" had fallen to his knees, sobbing.

He was a young man, about thirty, dressed in a labcoat and wearing horn-rimmed glasses. A computer nerd, but dirty, disheveled and terrified.

"Don't shoot! Please don't shoot! Oh my God, I'm so glad you're here! You have to help me! We lost control! They wouldn't obey us anymore! And then they—"

"Hold it, hold it," Schofield said, stepping forward. "Calm down. Start again. What's your name?"

"My n-name is . . . Pennebaker. Zak Pennebaker." He peered around fearfully.

Schofield saw that the name matched the one on the man's pocket-mounted ID badge. The ID badge also featured clearance levels and a silver disc at its base—an odd addition to a nametag. Schofield had never seen one before. *Radiation meter, perhaps?*

"I'm DARPA. High-end project. *Please,* you gotta get me outta here, off this boat, before they come back."

"Not until you tell us what this project was."

"I can't."

"Let me put it another way: you tell us about the project or we leave you here."

Zak Pennebaker didn't need three degrees to figure out that one. It came out in a blurting flurry.

"It started out as a super-soldier project, special ops stuff involving 'Go' drugs, amphetamines, biomechanics and brain-chip grafting. All on human subjects. But the human subjects didn't work out. The ape subjects, however, worked very, *very* well."

"*Ape* subjects?" Mother said in disbelief.

"Yes, apes. Gorillas. African mountain gorillas to be precise. They're twice as strong as human beings and the grafting technology worked perfectly with them."

"Not quite perfectly," Hulk said, indicating the state of the observation platform.

"Well, no, no, not in the end," Pennebaker mumbled. "But when the apes took so well to the tech, the project morphed from a special-forces operation to a frontline troop replacement project."

"What do you mean?" Schofield asked.

"The ultimate frontline trooper—lethal, vicious, remorseless, yet totally obedient. And best of all, totally *expendable.* No more letters from a grateful nation to grieving parents. No more one-legged veterans protesting in D.C. Hell, no more veterans full-stop—the government would save billions in entitlements alone. Imagine you're a general, facing a frontal assault, it's a lot easier to send a thousand purpose-bred apes to their deaths than fresh-faced farm boys from Idaho.

"And that's the best part, we bred the gorillas ourselves in labs, so we aren't even thinning the natural population, committing some crime against nature. They are the first custom-made artificially-produced armed force in the history of mankind. You could send them into hostile territory and they'd never question the order, you could send them on complete suicide missions and they'd never complain."

"How the hell do you manage that?" Hulk asked.

"The grafting technology," Schofield answered.

Pennebaker seemed surprised that Schofield would know about this. "Yes. That's correct."

"What's grafting technology?" Mother asked.

Schofield said, "You attach—or *graft*—a microchip to the brain of your subject. The chip is biomechanical, semi-organic, so it attaches to the brain and becomes part of it. Grafting technology has allowed quadriplegics to communicate via computers. Their brain engages with the chip and the chip sends a signal to the computer. *But* . . . I've heard it can also work the other way around . . ."

"That's right," Pennebaker said. "When an outside agent uses a grafted microchip to control *the subject*."

"Jesus, Mary and Joseph," Mother sighed. "Poin-

dexter, you musta read a million books in college filled with words I couldn't even understand, but didn't you just once think about reading *Frankenstein*?"

Pennebaker responded, "You have to believe me. The results were astonishing, at least at the start. The apes were perfectly obedient and shockingly effective. We taught them how to use weapons. We even created modified M-4 assault rifles for them, to accommodate their bigger hands. But even when they lost their guns, they were *still* hyper-effective—they could crush a man's head with their bare hands or bite his whole face off."

As Pennebaker spoke, Schofield stole a glance at his four men guarding the north-south catwalk. None of them had moved.

He keyed his UHF channel: "Astro? Hulk? Any contacts?"

"Not a thing from the north, sir."

"Ditto the south, sir. It's too quiet here."

Schofield turned back to Pennebaker. "You're saying you tested these things against human troops?"

Pennebaker bowed his head. "Yes. Against three companies of Marines that we had brought here from Okinawa. What are you guys?"

"Marines," Mother growled.

Pennebaker swallowed. "The apes annihilated them. Down on the battlefield and also on the island proper. Five hundred gorillas versus 600 Marines. It was a hell of a fight. The gorillas lost heaps in the opening exchange, but they just weathered the losses without a backward step. The chips in their heads don't allow for ineffective emotions like fear. So the apes just kept coming, climbing over the piles of their dead, until the Marines were toast."

Mother pushed her face—and pistol—into Pennebaker's. "You call a Marine *toast* again, fuck-nut, and I'll waste you right now."

Schofield said softly, "And fear is not an ineffective emotion, Mr. Pennebaker."

Pennebaker shrugged. "Whatever. You see, it was then the apes started doing . . . unexpected . . . things. Independent strategic thinking; killing their own wounded. And then there were the more *unseemly* things, like cutting the hands off their vanquished enemies and piling them up."

"Yeah, heard about that," Mother said. "Charming."

"And then they turned on you," Schofield said.

"And then they turned on us. The most unexpected thing of all. While we were looking the other way, observing the exercise, they sent a sub-team to take this tower. Took us by surprise. They're smart, *tactical*. They out-thought us and now they own this ship and the island. Marines, welcome to the end of your lives."

"We're not dead yet," Schofield said.

"Oh, yes you are. You're completely screwed," Pennebaker said. "You have to understand: *you can't beat these things.* They are stronger than you are. They are faster. Christ, they've been *bred* to fight for longer, to stay awake for ninety-six hours at a time—four days—so if they don't kill you straight away, they'll just wait you out and get you later, like they did with the last few regular Marines. Add to that, their technological advantages—Signet-5 radio-locaters, surgically-implanted digital headsets—and your headstones are practically engraved. These things are the *evolution* of the modern soldier, Captain, and they're so damned good, even their makers couldn't control them."

Mother shook her head. "How do you geniuses manage to keep doing things like this—?"

Without warning, a voice exploded in Schofield's earpiece: Astro's voice.

"Oh God no, we missed them! Shit! Captain! Duck!"

Standing with his back to the main hangar, Schofield didn't turn to verify Astro's warning.

He just obeyed, trusting his man, and dived to the floor—a bare instant before a black man-sized *creature* came swooping in over his head and slammed to the floor right where he'd been standing.

Had Schofield remained standing for even a nanosecond longer, the K-Bar knife in the creature's hand would have slashed his throat.

The creature now stood before him and for the briefest of moments Schofield got a look at it.

It was indeed an ape, perhaps five-and-a-half feet tall, with straggly black hair. But this was no ordinary jungle gorilla. It wore a lightweight helmet, from the front of which hung an orange visor that covered the animal's eyes. On the helmet's rear were some stubby antennas. Kevlar body armor covered its chest and shoulders. Wrist guards protected its arms. And in a holster on its back was a modified M-4.

Goddamn.

But that was all Schofield got to see, for right then the ape bared its jaws and launched itself at him—just as it was shot to bits, about a million bits, as Mother and Hulk nailed it with their MP-7s.

Then Astro yelled: *"Marines! Look sharp! They're not coming in via the catwalk! They're coming at you from across the ceiling!"*

Only now did Schofield stand and spin to check the ceiling of the hangar near his tower.

Coming across it, using the complex array of pipes, lights, pulleys and rails that lined the hangar's ceiling, was a phalanx of about forty black gorillas, all dressed like the dead one and moving across the super-high ceiling with ease.

And then Schofield's horror became complete as the nearest ape—hanging upside-down from three of its four limbs, raised its free hand, leveled an M-4 at the tower and opened fire.

SECOND ASSAULT

HELL ISLAND

1600 HOURS

1 AUGUST

THE APES moved across the ceiling with incredible speed, clambering across it faster than a human could run across land. And the fact that they were more than a hundred feet off the floor didn't seem to faze them at all.

Schofield's Marines opened fire and the first three gorillas dropped off the ceiling in explosions of blood, shrieking.

But the others just kept on coming, firing as they advanced.

The man beside Schofield, a young private known as Cheese, was hit square in the face and thrown backwards. Another Marine was hit in the chest and flopped to the floor.

Then the force of apes split and started to fan out around the tower, like an ocean wave washing around a rock.

Mother was busy unleashing a withering volley of fire at three of the incoming beasts when a fourth ape landed with a thud on the open window-ledge of the tower right next to her and threw itself at her from the side.

Ape and Marine went sprawling across the floor, struggling violently, desperately. Since both had lost their guns in the tumble, this would be the worst kind of battle: hand-to-hand, to the death.

Now Mother was strong but the ape was stronger and it quickly got the upper hand, head butting her hard and then throwing her against a nearby table. With a roar, the ape hurled itself at her, aiming its bared teeth at her nose . . .

. . . only to catch one of Mother's grenades in its mouth. Mother had whipped it around and jammed it into the creature's jaws.

"Get a taste of this," she said, releasing the spoon and rolling away a second before the gorilla's head simply exploded, transforming instantly into a shower of red spray.

The force of gorillas was now converging on the high tower from all sides, raining automatic fire on the Marines inside it—who returned that fire with interest.

Then the gorillas started leaping en masse down onto the tower's observation platform—in one instance, four of them crash-tackled one of Schofield's Marines, taking him down with their bare hands. One gorilla was ripped to shreds by the Marine's final spray of fire, but the rest got him. The hapless man fell screaming, covered by the frenzied apes.

Given the gorillas' suicidal frontal-assault strategy, their numbers dropped fast. Forty had quickly become twenty, but even then the numbers game was still in their favor: Schofield's ten-man Marine team was now down to seven, three on the tower, plus the four over on the catwalk supplying cover fire.

"Marines!" Schofield called. "Get off this tower! Back to the catwalk! Now!"

He began to retreat—pushing Zak Pennebaker in front of him—loosing three shots as he did so, dropping three gorillas that had just landed inside the tower. But the three apes didn't die; they clawed after him despite their wounds and it took *six more shots* to neutralize them all.

A gurgled scream as the Marine beside Schofield was shot in the throat. He fell, and even though he was already mortally wounded, two gorillas descended on him with a fury, firing their guns into his body, tearing at his face with their hands.

Jesus . . . Schofield's eyes went wide.

Of the six Marines who had stepped onto the tower, only he and Mother remained.

They retreated, with Pennebaker between them, back across the gangway-bridge to the long north-south catwalk, chased by the twenty gorillas.

Once on the catwalk, Schofield checked his options. The gorillas, still using the pipe-riddled ceiling as their means of travel, were angling toward the south end of the catwalk, leaving Schofield with only one choice.

"North," he ordered. "To the bow! Go!"

The six remaining Marines—Schofield, Mother,

Astro, Sanchez, Bigfoot and Hulk—charged along the catwalk, heading forward, their boots clanging on the walkway.

Seconds later, the gorillas arrived at the catwalk and started their pursuit, exchanging fire with the last man in the Marine squad, Sanchez.

The catwalk ended at an immense steel wall that bisected the hangar deck. The enormous hangar stretched for nearly the full length of the ship, but it was cut in the middle by this watertight wall, so if the carrier ever flooded, only one hangar bay would be lost.

Moving in the lead of her desperate fleeing team, Mother threw open a bulkhead door in the great wall, to reveal that the catwalk continued beyond it in a straight line, only now suspended over a second hangar bay, the forward one.

Mother froze in the doorway.

"God have mercy . . ." she breathed.

Schofield came up alongside her, looked beyond the doorway into the forward hangar bay.

"Oh . . . my . . . God . . ."

This hangar bay had no indoor battlefield, just regular planes, trucks and jeeps on its wide bare floor.

What it did have, however, were about 350 gorillas standing on the floor of the gigantic hangar bay, milling around the remains of Condor's 82nd Airborne unit.

Schofield looked down in time to see the lead ape

yank Condor's rifle from the Airborne leader's dead hands, raise it into the air and roar in triumph.

Then—Schofield didn't know how; it was almost as if it had a sixth sense—the lead ape turned and looked up and stared directly in Shane Schofield's eyes.

It was like stumbling into a lion's den while the lion was eating a meal.

The lead ape let out a loud roar and the crowd of gorillas around him moved at once in response: they started scaling every available ladder—some even scaled the giant dividing wall itself—heading for the catwalk on which Schofield's team now stood.

RUNNING IN the rear, Sanchez arrived at the doorway in the dividing wall just as Schofield came charging *back out* through it.

"What——?"

"Back this way," Schofield said, not even stopping.

"But they're still back there——"

"We've got a better chance against this group than that one." Schofield and the others shoved past Sanchez, heading back south, heading aft.

Ever doubtful, Sanchez *had* to look for himself—and he saw the multitude of apes surging up at him from the forward hangar bay. "Goddamn . . ."

"Sanchez!" Schofield called back. "When you decide to join us, lock that door behind you!"

Sanchez locked the door, then blew the lock for good measure, then turned and followed the others.

Schofield ran back down the high catwalk—having squeezed past his team until he was once again in the lead—now heading aft and once more confronted by the original smaller squad of gorillas.

"Mother! Astro! Bigfoot! Rolling leapfrog formation!" he called as he went by. "Full auto. Do it."

He was running full tilt now, MP-7 raised.

Running and firing down the catwalk, Schofield took down three of the twenty apes charging at him along the same walkway.

Once his gun went dry, he hit the deck, dropping to his belly, allowing Mother to hurdle him and do the same—run and fire with a fury.

She nailed six more, then dropped to *her* belly . . . at which point Astro hurdled her, guns blazing.

Then Astro ducked and Bigfoot hurdled him, and thus the four of them took down the small gorilla force in a textbook turnaround maneuver, and suddenly they were alone in the vast space.

Not for long.

The larger gorilla force had started banging on the door in the dividing wall. Then, with a loud mechanical groaning, a large vehicle-access door down on the floor began to roll upwards, opening . . .

"Scarecrow! What do we do!" Mother yelled. "I've never been in this kind of situation before!"

"We stay alive, any way we can! *There*!"

He pointed at the aft-most elevator on the starboard side of the hangar. It was a giant thing, a huge hydraulic open-air platform that hung off the side of the carrier, designed to lift entire planes from the hangar deck up to the flight deck.

Today, a gangway branched off the outer edge of

the massive elevator, stretching down to the dock of Hell Island.

"The gangway!" Schofield called. "Go!"

The six-man Marine team reached a long ladder that connected the high catwalk to the floor of the hangar, slid down it one after the other, Schofield leading the way.

The main gorilla force was now flooding into the aft hangar bay like bats out of hell. Their numbers were incredible, they literally *poured* through the access door from the forward hangar, then clambered over the muddy fake battlefield, climbing up and over the trenches and barbed wire, guns firing, teeth bared.

It was, quite simply, the most fearsome assault force Schofield had ever seen.

Armed, enraged, and completely lacking the fear of death—any human force that saw these things bearing down on it would in all likelihood just go to water.

Schofield was almost at the exterior elevator, only fifty yards away, when something completely unexpected happened.

The elevator began to rise.

"Oh no . . . *no* . . ."

The great platform lifted fast, taking the gangway with it. As the elevator rose up and out of sight, heading for the flight deck, the gangway leading to dry land dropped down into the water with an ungainly splash.

"They—" Bigfoot gasped. "Son of a bitch . . ."

"Next plan?" Sanchez said.

"Stay moving." Schofield scanned the area for another escape. "Always stay moving. While you're moving, you're still in the game. If you stop, you're dead. Never stop."

As he spoke, he saw two large transport trucks parked over by the wall. "Those trucks! Get in and make for the flight deck!"

The squad split up, racing for the two trucks. They were five-ton troop transports, with high canvas awnings covering their rear trays.

Schofield and Bigfoot dived into the cab of one truck; Mother, Astro, Hulk and Sanchez jumped into the other one.

As Schofield slid into the driver's seat, he spun to check on the scientist, Pennebaker, to see if he was keeping up—

—only to see Zak Pennebaker skulking into a side door of the hangar thirty yards away, *on his own,* preferring, it seemed, to handle this disaster by himself. He disappeared through the door.

"What the—?" Schofield frowned. But he didn't have time to ponder the issue. The apes had cleared the battlefield and were now advancing across the open deck like the army of darkness.

Schofield gunned the engine.

*   *   *

The two trucks roared to life, shot off the mark, heading for the upward-spiraling vehicle ramp that led to the flight deck—a journey that involved briefly driving *back toward* the ape army and racing the oncoming army to the ramp's wide doorway roughly halfway between the two forces.

It was a dead-heat. Mother's truck reached the ramp's doorway just as the ape force did.

The first gorillas launched themselves at her truck, clutching onto any handhold they could find, just as it sped inside the rampway. Eight of them got a grip on it.

It was worse for Schofield.

Driving behind Mother, he got to the ramp entrance two seconds too late. The ape army swarmed across the doorway, blocking it, and suddenly he had a decision to make: plough through the mass of hairy black beasts, or turn away.

Screw it.

He ploughed right into the seething horde of apes, slamming through their ranks with his big five-ton truck.

Squeals, shrieks . . . and gunfire as the apes opened fire.

A barrage of bullets shattered Schofield's windshield—apes went flying left and right—some banging against the truck's bullbar, others disappearing under it, more still grabbing onto its sides and climbing aboard it—the truck bumping and bouncing.

Schofield ducked as gunfire assaulted his cab, slamming into the headrest of his seat.

It was too much fire. Driving head-on toward it, he couldn't keep control of the truck. He couldn't get to the rampway.

He yanked on the steering wheel, veered away from the ape-filled doorway . . . now with no less than twenty-five apes hanging from his truck!

The truck swung in a wide circle away from the rampway, across the open area of clear deck-space at the southern end of the hangar.

Suddenly, with a roar, an ape bounced down onto the bonnet of the truck and *blam!* Schofield nailed it with one of his two .45 caliber Desert Eagle pistols, throwing the creature off the truck.

Then another ape swung in *through* the driver's side window with its gun raised and—*blam!*— Bigfoot fired across Schofield's body, sending the gorilla flying away with a yelp.

Then two more apes hung down from the roof of the cab—their heads appearing upside-down, with their M-4s extended—only for Schofield to fire repeatedly up into the *ceiling* of the cab, hitting the two apes in their chests through the metal of the roof! The pair of apes convulsed violently before sliding off the speeding truck.

"Boss! We can't keep this up!" Bigfoot called. "It's only a matter of time till they overwhelm us!"

"I know! I know!" Schofield yelled back, searching for an option.

The big truck swung in its wild circle, absolutely

covered by gorillas, flinging some of them clear with the centrifugal force.

Then Schofield saw the *port*-side exterior elevator.

It was on the ocean side of the ship. Right now, on it was an F-14 Tomcat fighter jet, attached to a low towing vehicle.

Schofield's eyes lit up. "Hang on." He gunned the engine and broke out of his circular line of travel, cutting a beeline for the port-side elevator.

"What are you doing!"

"Just get ready to jump . . ."

They hit the open-air elevator doing sixty, just as two more gorillas jumped down onto the truck's running boards and *wrenched off* the doors on either side of the cab—only to be blown away a second later by Schofield and Bigfoot firing across each other.

"Now!" Schofield yelled . . .

. . . and he and Bigfoot dived out of the speeding truck, landing in twin rolls on either side of it . . .

. . . while the truck continued straight on and shot off the edge of the exterior elevator, sailing through the air, wheels spinning, still covered in a mass of black gorillas, before it crashed down into the sea with a gigantic splash.

Schofield and Bigfoot lay on the open-air elevator, gasping for breath.

"You okay?" Schofield asked. "Still got all your limbs?"

"Uh, yeah, I think so . . ."

Schofield spun, to see the full ape army staring at him from the other side of the hangar, eighty yards away.

They roared as one and charged.

"Oh, Christ . . ."

AT THE same time as Schofield was sending his truck to a watery grave, Mother's truck was sweeping up the access ramp to the flight deck, bearing eight apes on its roof and outer flanks, and being chased by about a hundred more *on foot*.

It was like escaping from the underworld, pursued by all of its demons.

Mother floored it, slamming the ascending truck into the outer walls of the spiraling ramp-way, losing a couple of apes that way.

In the tray at the back of the truck, Sanchez, Astro and Hulk were doing battle with four apes that had just swung inside.

Sanchez shot one in the chest, while Astro disarmed another and kicked it through the side canvas of the truck, but Hulk wasn't so lucky. The other two apes took him on together, and in the scuffle one managed to shoot him in the stomach.

Hulk roared in pain—just as the two apes did something totally unexpected: they yanked him off the back of the speeding truck, jumping with him, without any thought, it seemed, to the injuries they themselves would suffer.

Astro saw it all in a kind of surreal slow motion.

He saw Hulk's eyes go wide as the big man fell to the ramp behind the upwardly-racing truck, gripped by the two gorillas.

Then he saw the onrushing army of apes overwhelm Hulk, choosing to use their M-4s as clubs rather than guns. Astro winced as he lost sight of Hulk amid the mass of black hair.

But even then, not every ape stopped to join in the mauling of Hulk—the rest just kept running, clambering around the gorillas battering Hulk's body, still chasing the fleeing truck.

"Jesus . . ." Astro breathed.

And then *wham!* Mother's truck burst into gray daylight, into the pouring rain assaulting the flight deck. Uncountable raindrops hammered its windshield.

The four remaining gorillas on the truck made their move.

They converged on the cab in a coordinated manner—swinging down together from the roof, one arriving at each door, the other two landing on the bonnet of the truck, right in front of Mother, guns up.

"Yikes . . ." Mother breathed.

There was no escape. No chance.

Except . . .

"Hang on, boys!" she called into her UHF radio.

And with that, she yanked on the steering wheel, bringing the truck into a sharp right-hand turn, a turn that was far too fast for a vehicle of its type.

Gravity played its part.

The truck turned sharply . . . its inner wheels lifting off the tarmac . . . and it rolled.

The big truck tumbled across the rain-slicked flight deck, sending the apes on its cab and bonnet flying in every direction. Then it landed on its side and slid for a full sixty feet before coming to rest against the lone Super Stallion helicopter on the deck.

Mother clambered out of the overturned truck, raced to its rear.

"You okay?" she called, crouching to her knees.

Sanchez and Astro lay crumpled against the side wall of the tray, bruised and bloody but alive.

"Come on," Mother peered back at the ramp. "We gotta keep—"

She cut herself off.

The apes were already at the top of the ramp.

A great crowd of them—easily one hundred strong—now stood on the deck, in the rain, at the entrance to the ramp, grunting and snorting and glaring right at her.

STILL ON her knees, totally exposed, Mother just sighed.

"Game over. We lose."

The apes charged, raising their guns, pulling the triggers.

Mother shut her eyes.

The sound of gunfire rang out—loud, hard and brutal—and Mother imagined this was the last sound she'd ever hear.

Braaaaaaaaaaaaap!

But there was something wrong with this sound.

It was *too loud* for an M-4, too deep. It was the sound of a much larger gun.

Crouched at the rear of her overturned truck, Mother had never noticed the port-side elevator rise up to deck-level behind her.

Never saw what stood *on* the open-air elevator: an F-14 Tomcat, pointed right at her.

And in the cockpit of the Tomcat . . .

. . . were Shane Schofield and Bigfoot!

Schofield sat in the pilot's seat, gripping the control stick and jamming down on its trigger.

Sizzling tracer rounds whizzed by Mother on either side, popping past her ears, before razing into the crowd of gorillas beyond her, mowing them down.

The first three rows of gorillas fell at once. The others split up, fanned out, sought cover.

"Mother!" Schofield's voice said in her ear. *"Get out of here! I'll hold them off!"*

"Where can we go?" Mother dragged Astro out of the truck and started running, with Sanchez by her side.

"Get to Casper's door!" Schofield said cryptically. *"Go over the stern! I'll meet you there!"*

Mother did as she was told, hustling to the rear edge of the deck, where she lowered Astro over the side, down to a safety net just below the edge. She and Sanchez then jumped down after him and disappeared inside a hatch.

That left Schofield and Bigfoot in the Tomcat on the port-side elevator, facing the now 80-strong force of apes.

"Bigfoot! Let's move! Time to get out of here—"

All of a sudden, their fighter started rocking wildly.

Schofield spun in his seat. "Shit! They must have climbed up the side of the ship!"

The rest of the ape army—nearly 300 gorillas—was now climbing *up and over the outer edges of the elevator platform!*

They swarmed around the plane, clambered up onto it, shook it, hit it, fired at it.

Schofield closed the Tomcat's canopy a split second before it was hit by gunfire. Made of reinforced Lexan glass, the canopy was capable of deflecting high-velocity air-to-air tracers, so it could handle this small-arms fire, even from up close.

But then one clever gorilla climbed into the towing vehicle that was attached to the Tomcat and started it up.

"Aw, no way, that just ain't fair . . ." Bigfoot breathed.

Covered in rampaging apes and now pulled by the towing vehicle, the Tomcat slowly started moving . . .

. . . toward the edge of the elevator!

"They're going to tip us over the side!" Bigfoot exclaimed.

Indeed they were.

The Tomcat rolled toward the edge of the elevator, six stories above the waterline.

As it did so, the apes on its back started bailing off it, jumping clear. They knew what was about to happen.

"Ah, Captain . . ." Bigfoot said. "Any ideas?"

"Yeah. Buckle up." Schofield was already strapping on his seatbelt.

"Buckle up? How's that going to—oh!" Bigfoot clutched at his belts, started clasping them.

The towing vehicle came to the edge of the platform and the ape driving it bailed out just as the towing vehicle tipped over the edge, now hanging from the Tomcat's front landing gear.

The ape army did the rest. They pushed the F-14 until its front wheels lurched off the edge and the entire plane—with Schofield and Bigfoot in it—fell, off the carrier, plunging ninety feet *straight down* to the water far below.

THE INSTANT the Tomcat fell off the edge, the canopy of the fighter blew open and the F-14's two ejection seats shot up out of the plane.

The ejection seats—with Schofield and Bigfoot on them—rocketed up into the sky above the aircraft carrier while the Tomcat went in the opposite direction, the plane falling in a clumsy tumbling heap down the side of the boat and into the water, where it landed with a great splash and immediately began to sink.

Schofield and Bigfoot flew high into the air before they disengaged their flight seats and initiated the parachutes that were attached to their seatbelts.

As the two of them floated back down to the earth, they scanned the huge force of apes on the deck of the carrier. They looked like an army of ants swarming over the aft runway.

Then suddenly Hail Mary gunshots started to zing past Schofield's head, tearing through his chute.

"Where to now?" Bigfoot asked over the UHF.

Schofield pursed his lips, thinking fast. His eyes fell on the chunky CH-53 Super Stallion in the center of the flight deck.

"It's time to even the score a little. Follow me."

He angled his gliding flight back toward the carrier, toward its mid-section.

Schofield touched down on the middle of the flight deck. Bigfoot landed a second after him, not far from the catapult launch controls.

The apes charged forward, roaring, firing, rampaging.

"Stay here," Schofield ordered before racing across the open deck to the massive Super Stallion.

Hunched in the pouring rain, he did something near the front of the chopper out of Bigfoot's sight before he came back around and charged into the chopper via its forward right-side door, slamming the door shut an instant before the gorillas arrived, banging on the side of the chopper, massing around it.

Inside the Super Stallion, Schofield hustled into the cockpit, shutting its door behind him, locking it.

Watching from the outside, taking cover behind the on-deck launch controls, Bigfoot was confused.

What was Schofield doing?

But then something even more confusing occurred.

The rear loading ramp of the Super Stallion folded open.

Naturally, the apes stormed it, fifty of them rushing inside, hungry for Schofield's blood.

Bigfoot frowned. *What on earth is he . . . ?*

"Bigfoot!" Schofield's voice said over the UHF. *"After you do what I ask, get down to Casper's door and find the others. I'll meet you there."*

"Casper's d—? Oh yeah, sure," Bigfoot said. "But what do you want me to do now?"

"Simple. Initiate Catapult No. 1."

"What—!"

At that moment, Schofield brought the rear loading ramp back up, closing it, *trapping* the fifty-odd apes that had gone inside.

It was then that Bigfoot saw what Schofield had done at the *front* of the chopper: via a tie-down chain, Schofield had attached the helicopter to the carrier's No. 1 launch catapult.

"You have got to be kidding . . ." Bigfoot said.

"Uh, now please, Bigfoot. They're about to break down the cockpit door."

"Right."

Bigfoot hit a switch on the launch console, igniting Catapult No. 1.

The Super Stallion hurtled down the length of the runway at a speed no helicopter had gone before.

The steam-driven catapult slingshot it down the tarmac at an astonishing 160 km/h!

The great chopper's landing wheels snapped off

after about ninety feet and the CH-53 *slid* the rest of the way, *on its belly,* sparks flying everywhere, the ear-piercing shriek of metal scraping against the flight deck filling the air.

And then . . . *shoom* . . . the Super Stallion shot off the bow of the *Nimitz,* soaring out horizontally from the flight deck for a full 150 feet, hanging in the air for a moment before it arced downward, falling toward the sea.

A second before it hit the ocean, a human figure could be seen leaping from one of its cockpit windows, jumping clear of the falling helicopter, hitting the water at the same time it did, but safely alongside it.

The helicopter came down with a massive splash and as the splash subsided, it could be seen bobbing slowly in the water.

And then it began to sink.

Shrieks could be heard from within it—the cries of the trapped gorillas.

Ten seconds later, the Super Stallion went under, with its cargo of murderous apes, never to rise again.

Shane Schofield trod water for a few moments, staring at what he'd just done. Then he started swimming back toward the ship, heading for the bow.

Once there, he pulled a Pony bottle from his combat webbing—a compact bottle-sized SCUBA tank fitted with a mouthpiece. He jammed it into his mouth and went underwater.

Within a minute, he arrived at a little-known entrance to the carrier, one located fifty feet below the waterline: a submarine docking door.

Designed to recover long-range reconnaissance troops—read spies—returning to the *Nimitz* via small submarines, for a long time Marines had referred to it as the spooks' door. Over time, "spook" had become "ghost" and then ghost had become "Casper," as in the friendly one.

This was Casper's door.

Schofield knocked loudly on it—in Morse code, punching out: "Mother. You there?"

At first there was no reply and Schofield's heart began to beat a little faster, before suddenly there came a muffled answering knock from the other side:

"As always."

THIRD ASSAULT

HELL ISLAND

1745 HOURS

1 AUGUST

SCHOFIELD'S TEAM sat in a grim silent circle beside the airlock that was Casper's door, deep within the bowels of the carrier.

There were only five of them now.

Schofield, Mother, Sanchez, Bigfoot and Astro.

Schofield sat on his own a short distance from the other four, head bowed, deep in thought . . . and dripping wet. He'd taken his anti-flash glasses off and was rubbing his scar-cut eyes.

"What the hell are we gonna do?" Sanchez moaned. "We're on an island in the middle of the biggest ocean in the world, with three hundred of those *things* hunting us down. We're completely, utterly, abso-fuckin-lutely screwed."

Astro shook his head. "There's just too many of them. It's only a matter of time."

Mother looked over at Schofield—still sitting with his head bent, thinking.

The others followed her gaze, as if waiting for him to say something.

Sanchez misunderstood Schofield's silence for fear.

"Aw, great! He's *frozen up!* Man, I wish I coulda stayed in the Buck's unit."

"Hey!" Mother barked. "I've had a gutful of your griping, Sanchez. You doubt the Scarecrow one more time and I'll perform my own court martial on you right here. That man's got the coolest head in the game. Cooler than the fucking Buck and way cooler than you, that's for sure. I've seen him think his way out of worse situations than this."

"Pancho," Bigfoot said softly. "She's right. You shoulda seen him up on the flight deck. He must have taken out forty of those apes from the Tomcat, and then another fifty in the chopper that he tossed off the bow. He's taken care of ninety of them all by himself. Now, I know you liked serving with the Buck, but you gotta move on. This guy's not better or worse than the Buck, he's just different. Why don't you cut him a break."

This was a big moment. Bigfoot was Sanchez's closest friend in the unit, his former teammate under "Buccaneer" Broyles.

Sanchez scowled. "I got a question then. In R7, in Florida, back in '04, the Buck beat everybody except him." He jerked a nod at Schofield. "Led by him, you guys evaded us for forty-one hours, till the exercise was over. How did you guys do that for so long?"

Mother indicated Schofield: "It was all him, all his doing. He saw a pattern in the Buck's moves, and once he found that pattern, he could anticipate every move you guys made. You had a numerical advantage, but since he could predict your every next move, it didn't matter."

"What pattern did he see in our moves?"

"Scarecrow realized that the Buck employed the same tactic repeatedly: he'd always use one sub-team to push his opponent toward a larger, waiting, force. You see, that's Scarecrow's biggest talent. He spots patterns, the enemy's patterns, their tactics and strategies . . . and then he uses those patterns against them."

"But he didn't use anything against us in R7," Sanchez said. "He just avoided us. He didn't *hurt* us in any way."

"Oh, yes, he did," Mother said. "By evading you guys till the end of the ex, he deprived you of the one thing you wanted most of all: a clear win."

Sanchez growled. This was true.

Her point made, Mother turned to look back at Schofield—

—only to find him gazing directly back at her, his eyes alive.

She said, "Well, hey there, handsome. What's up? Whatcha thinking?"

It was as if a lightbulb had lit up above his head.

"The Buck . . ." he said.

"What about him?"

"He's here. Now. Commanding these ape troops."

SCHOFIELD SPOKE quickly.

"Think back. In the observation tower above the indoor battlefield, the apes on the ceiling drove us *forward,* toward the other force of apes in the forward hangar. The *larger* force.

"Then in the aft hangar, they let us try for the portside elevator but then removed it, knowing we'd have to come *back* through their larger force. They were always driving us toward the larger numbers. It would also explain why the Corps disbanded the Buck's unit a few months ago—he was being assigned to a special mission. This one."

Astro said, "But that scientist, Pennebaker, said the exercise had gone pear-shaped. If the Buck was here, he'd be dead, too, killed by the gorillas."

"And where's Pennebaker now?" Schofield asked. "He was last seen ditching us in the aft hangar, during the gorillas' main assault. Either he felt he was safer on his own—unlikely—or he was part of something bigger, a messenger sent to give us information. Mother, gentlemen, I'm not convinced the 'exercise' here at Hell Island went pear-shaped at all. In fact,

I'm starting to wonder if it's still going . . . and we're a part of it."

There was a silence.

Sanchez said, "Okay. So if the Buck's here, where is he?"

"Somewhere on the boat?" Astro suggested.

"No, I don't think so," Schofield swapped a look with Mother. "The power drain."

Mother nodded. "Concur."

"What are you two talking about?" Sanchez asked.

Schofield said, "Back on the bridge, we detected a power drain going off the ship and onto the island. The Buck—and whoever else is controlling this ape army—is somewhere on Hell Island."

He stood, putting his silver anti-flash glasses back on, now looking more lethal than ever.

"Knowledge is a wonderful thing. Now that we've figured some of this out, it's time to turn the tables."

SCHOFIELD WAITED till dusk to leave the *Nimitz*.

If he was going to take on the island, the cover of darkness would be necessary. It also gave him a chance to do some research.

He dispatched Mother and Astro to find any maps of Hell Island. They found some in a stateroom, ever aware of the howls of the gorillas searching the ship for them.

When they returned, Schofield and his team pored over the maps. The most helpful one showed a network of underground tunnels running throughout the island:

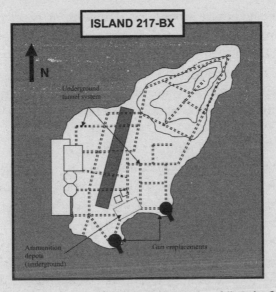

ISLAND 217-BX

N

Underground
tunnel system

Ammunition
depots
(underground)

Gun emplacements

"This used to be called Grant Island," Schofield said. "Until we stormed it in 1943 and removed it from all maps, so it could be used as a secret staging post. The fighting here was some of the fiercest of the war, almost as bad as Okinawa and Iwo Jima. Two thousand Japanese defenders fought to the very end on Grant, not giving a single inch—not wanting to give up its airfield. We lost eight hundred Marines taking it. Thing was, we almost lost a lot more."

"What do you mean?" Mother asked.

"Like Okinawa and Iwo Jima, Hell Island was honeycombed with tunnels—concrete tunnels that the Japanese built over two years, connecting all its gun emplacements, pillboxes, and ammo dumps. The Japanese could move around the island unseen, popping up from hidden holes and firing at point-blank range before disappearing again.

"But the tunnels on Hell Island had one extra purpose. They had a feature not seen anywhere else in the Pacific war: a flooding valve system."

"What was that?"

"It was the ultimate suicide ploy. If the island was taken, the last remaining Japanese officers were to retreat to the lowest underground ammunition chamber—presumably followed by the American forces. From that chamber, the Japanese could seal off the entire tunnel system and then open two huge ocean gates—floodgates built into the walls of the system that could let the ocean in. The system would flood, killing both the Japanese and all the Americans now trapped inside. Kind of like a final 'Screw you' to the victorious American force."

"Did the Japs use those gates in '43?" Sanchez asked.

"They did. But a small team of special-mission Marines braved the rising waters and using primitive breathing apparatus managed to close the ocean gates, saving five hundred Marines."

"How do you know this?" Bigfoot asked.

Schofield smiled weakly. "My grandfather was a member of that special team. His name was Lieutenant Michael Schofield. He led the team that held back the ocean."

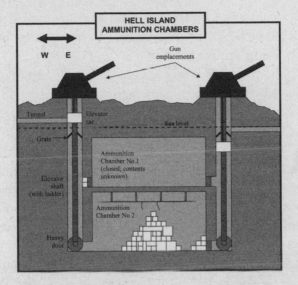

Schofield leaned back, staring at the map.

"The ammunition chambers . . ." he said. "If they're like other World War II-era chambers, they're big, hall-sized caverns. If we could lure the apes into one of them, we could seal them *all* inside and—hmmm . . ."

"What about finding the Buck and whoever else is behind this?" Sanchez said.

"Too risky. They could be anywhere on the island. They *are* also currently trying to kill us. No. We've been on the back foot all day. It's time we got proactive, it's time *we* set the agenda. And the way I see it, if we can pull this off," Schofield said, "maybe they'll find us. So what do you say, folks. Want to become gorilla bait?"

A T EXACTLY six p.m., the five Marines exited the *Nimitz* via the submarine docking door, swam over to the nearby shore and for the first time that day, set foot on Hell Island. The *Nimitz* loomed above them in the darkness, a dark shadow against the evening sky.

Schofield and his team quickly found an entrance to the underground tunnel system—a sixty-year-old cracked concrete archway that stank of decay, dust and the fearful sweat of soldiers long gone.

Inky darkness loomed beyond the old concrete arch.

Before they entered the tunnel network, Schofield stopped them.

"Okay, hold here for a moment. There's only one way this can work, and that's if they're right behind us."

He reached for his throat-mike and pressed "Transmit," opening up his regular radio channel.

"But they'll know where we are . . ." Astro said, alarmed.

"That's the whole point, kiddo," Mother said.

Schofield keyed his radio, put on a worried voice:

"Delta Leader, come in! Flash . . . Flash Gordon! You still alive out there? This is Scarecrow. Please respond!"

He received no reply from the Delta team.

But he did get another kind of response.

A terrifying howl echoed out from the flight deck of the *Nimitz*.

His transmission had been detected.

The gorillas were coming.

And they didn't take long getting there.

They swarmed off the *Nimitz*, an army of fast-moving shadows.

Zeroing in on Schofield's radio signal, the three hundred apes converged on the tunnel entrance, howling and roaring.

Schofield's team charged into the tunnel system, pursued by the monsters. It was scary enough moving through the dank concrete passageways—but doing it with an army of deadly creatures on your tail was even worse.

"This way," Schofield said, referring to his map.

He was heading for the two massive gun emplacements of Hell Island. The two big guns—twelve-inch behemoths—were positioned on a pair of cliffs pointing east and south, designed to ward off any approaching fleet.

Actually, that wasn't entirely correct: he was heading for the ammunition chambers buried *underneath and in between* the gun emplacements.

Through the tunnels they ran.

The gorillas caught up, firing and roaring. Schofield's team fired behind themselves as they ran, picking off the apes, never slowing down. To slow down was to die.

Then abruptly they came to a freight elevator.

"This is it. We're beneath the first gun emplacement," Schofield said. "This elevator was used to feed ammunition to the guns from the chambers down below."

Like the concrete world around it, the elevator was old and clunky, rusted beyond repair. It didn't work, but that didn't matter.

"Quickly, down," Schofield ordered.

One after the other, they swept down a rusty ladder that ran down the elevator shaft.

Moving last of all, Mother grabbed the ladder just as an ape came leaping out of the darkness, grabbing her gun-hand.

She pivoted on the ladder and hurled the gorilla free—allowing it to take her gun, but flinging it out into the elevator shaft. The gorilla sailed down the shaft, disappearing into blackness, its shriek ending with a dull thud somewhere down there.

"Hurry up, people!" Mother called downward.

They hustled down the ladder.

On the way, Schofield found a huge iron door set

into an alcove. Its Japanese markings had been painted over with English: ORDNANCE CHAMBER ONE.

Unfortunately, access to the door itself was obstructed by a cluster of heavy crates and boxes. They'd never get to it.

Down another level and they came to the bottom of the elevator shaft. Here Schofield found a second huge iron door marked ORDNANCE CHAMBER TWO. Not only was it free of obstructing crates, it was unlocked. Also here was a large circular pressure door that looked like the entry to a giant safe. It was easily ten feet in diameter.

Schofield ignored this circular door, pushed open the heavy iron door to the ordnance chamber and pulled a glow stick from his belt.

Beside him, Sanchez extracted a flare gun and raised it.

"No," Schofield said sharply. "Not here."

He cracked the glow stick—illuminating the room around them with its haunting amber glow—and suddenly Sanchez saw the wisdom of Schofield's words.

The room around them was enormous, high-ceilinged and concrete-walled, with floor space roughly the size of a basketball court. A network of overhead rails ran along its ceiling, dangling chains and hooks. An identical door lay on the far side, leading to a second elevator shaft that fed the other gun emplacement.

And piled up in its center, like an artificial mountain sixty feet tall, was a pyramid-shaped stack of wooden crates. Each crate was marked in either Japanese or English with DANGER: EXPLOSIVES or DANGER: FLAMMABLE. NO NAKED FLAMES.

In fact, Schofield couldn't recall seeing the word "danger" so many times in the one place.

"This is what we wanted," he said in a low voice. "Come on."

His team hustled inside.

THE APES arrived at the second ammunition chamber a minute later.

The first few must have been recon troops—for the first time that day they were cautious, checking things out, as if suspecting a trap.

They saw Schofield and Mother clambering up the mountain of wooden crates, heading for a catwalk near the ceiling—presumably to join the others up there, although they couldn't be seen. The recon gorillas ducked back outside, to report back to the others.

Thirty seconds later, the onslaught came.

It was spectacular in its ferocity.

The ape army *thundered* into the ammo chamber in full assault mode.

Screaming and shrieking, moving fast and spreading out, they stormed the subterranean hall—not firing. The scouts had informed the others of the flammable contents of the hall. They'd have to do this *without* guns.

The ape army leapt onto the mountain of crates,

coming after Schofield and Mother with a vengeance, coming to finish them off.

Schofield and Mother stayed at the peak of the crate mountain, each holding two MP-7 submachine guns and firing them with precision, aiming carefully to avoid hitting the ordnance all around them, taking down apes left, right and center.

Gunfire clattering.

Apes screaming and falling.

Muzzle flashes.

Two against an army.

And the apes just kept coming, live ones just clambering over the dead ones, scaling the artificial mountain. For every rank of gorillas that Schofield and Mother mowed down, another *two ranks* stepped forward.

Soon the mountain of crates was crawling with hairy black shapes, all scrambling in a fury for the two defiant Marines at the summit.

"Scarecrow . . . !" Mother called.

"Not yet! We have to wait till they're all inside . . . !"

Then the last apes entered the great underground room, and Schofield called, "Now!"

As he yelled, the first gorillas reached the summit and clutched at his boots—only to be completely surprised when Schofield and Mother suddenly discarded their guns and leapt *upward,* grabbing a pair of chains hanging from the ceiling-mounted rail network and using them to swing across the length of the chamber, high above the army of apes swarming over the crate-mountain.

Schofield and Mother hit the western wall of the hall and unclipped clasps on their chains—causing the chains to unreel from the ceiling, lowering the two of them to the floor of the room right in front of the doorway leading back to the elevator shaft.

"Marines! Now!"

It was then that the other three members of Schofield's unit revealed themselves—from *behind* some crates near the entrance to the ammunition chamber. They all stepped back out through the heavy entry door, and raised their guns to fire back in through the gap.

And suddenly the trap became clear.

The *entire* gorilla army was now inside the one enclosed space, swarming all over the most combustible mountain in history.

And with Schofield and Mother now down and safe, Bigfoot, Astro and Sanchez aimed their guns at the base of the mountain of crates.

"Fire!" Schofield commanded.

They squeezed their triggers.

But then, from completely out of nowhere, a voice called: *"Captain Schofield! Don't!"*

SCHOFIELD SNAPPED up. "Marines! Hold that order! Do not fire!"

The voice—it was a man's voice—was desperate and pleading. It echoed out from ancient loudspeakers positioned around the great concrete room and inside the elevator shaft.

By this time the apes had started descending the mountain of crates, coming back down after Schofield and Mother, but then the voice addressed them:

"Troops! Desist and stand down!"

Immediately, the apes stopped where they stood, sitting down on their haunches in total and absolute obedience.

What had moments before been a frenzied blood-hungry army of apes was now a perfectly-behaved crowd of three hundred silent mountain gorillas.

And then suddenly *people* appeared behind Schofield's team, moving slowly and calmly, stepping down from the ladder in the elevator shaft: seven men in lab-coats, one officer in uniform, and covering them, a team of Delta commandos: the same ten-man team led by Hugh "Flash" Gordon that had parachuted in with Schofield's unit earlier that day.

Among the scientists in the lab-coats, Schofield recognized Zak Pennebaker, the "desperate" scientist he'd met earlier.

He also recognized the officer in uniform, which happened to be the khaki day uniform of the United States Marine Corps. He was Captain William "Buccaneer" Broyles, a.k.a. the Buck.

The leader of the lab-coated crowd stepped forward. He was an older man, with a mane of flowing white hair, an aged crinkled face, and dazzling blue eyes. He oozed authority.

"Captain Schofield," he said in a deep voice. "Thank you for your quick response to my plea. My name is Dr. Malcolm Knox, scientific consultant to the President, head of the Special Warfare Division at DARPA and overall commander of *Project Stormtrooper.*"

Knox walked out among the apes—they continued to sit obediently, although they did rock from side to side, fidgeting impatiently. But they did not attack him. Schofield noticed a silver disc on Knox's ID badge—it was exactly the same as the one Pennebaker had been wearing earlier and, Schofield saw, was still wearing now.

Standing with the apes at his back, Knox turned to Schofield and his dirty, blood-covered team.

"Congratulations. You have won this mission, Captain Schofield," he said.

Schofield said nothing.

"I said, you *won,*" Knox said. "I commend you on an incredible effort. Indeed, yours was the only team to survive."

Still Schofield remained silent.

Knox stammered. "You really, er, should all be proud—"

"This was a goddamned test," Schofield said in a low voice, his tone deadly.

"Yes . . . yes, it was," Knox said, slightly unnerved. "The final test of a new technology—"

Schofield said, "You pitted your new army against three companies of Marines, and you beat them. But then the higher-ups said you had to beat Special Forces, didn't they?"

Knox nodded. "This is correct."

"So you had us parachuted in here, with the SEALs and the Airborne. You used us as *live bait.* You used us as human guinea pigs for a *test*—"

"This gorilla force could save thousands of American lives in future conflicts," Knox said. "You, Captain Schofield, are sworn to defend the American people and your fellow soldiers. You were doing exactly that, only in an indirect way."

"In an indirect way . . ." Schofield growled. "I've lost five good men here today, Dr. Knox. Not to men-

tion the other Marines, SEALs and Airbornes who also died here in your little experiment. These men had families. They were prepared to die for their country fighting its *enemies,* not its latest fucking weapon."

"Sometimes a few must be lost for the greater good, Captain," Knox said. "This is bigger than you. This is the future of warfare for our country."

"But your apes *lost* in the end. We had them in the crosshairs and were about to fire the kill-shot."

"Yes, you did. You most certainly did," Knox said. "Your participation in this exercise was requested for precisely that reason: your adaptability and unpredictability. The apes needed such an adversary.

"As it stands, however, the gorillas beat everybody but you, and your victory, it must be said, was based in large part on a few longshots, in particular a level of knowledge that 99 percent of our enemies simply will not have: submarine docking doors in carriers and an unusually high level of knowledge of World War II Japanese tunnel systems. No, based on the results of this test, *Project Stormtrooper* will most certainly go live, and it will save many lives over the years to come."

Knox started walking around the hall, checking the apes. "Now, if you don't mind, we have a lot of follow-up to do and a whole lot of paperwork. An extraction plane has been called from Okinawa to come and take you home. It should be here in a few hours."

"Paperwork . . ." Schofield said. "Men have died

and you have paperwork. You guys are something else. Hey, hold it. I have another question."

Knox stopped.

Schofield nodded at Flash Gordon and the Delta team arrayed around him. "Why were *they* brought here at all, if they just stayed with you?"

Knox grinned. "They were brought in for my DARPA team's protection. Just in case you *did* happen to survive and got angry with us."

Knox resumed his casual appraisal of his apes.

Schofield said, "I should have offed your army when I had the chance."

"No, you shouldn't have, Captain. What you should do is walk away and be proud of yourself. You have done future generations of American farm boys a great service. They will not need to die on the front lines *ever* again. Also, be proud that my apes defeated every other force they faced, but *you* beat *them*. Go home."

"This is not right. It shouldn't be done this way," Schofield said.

"What you think, Captain, is unimportant and irrelevant. You are not paid to think about such weighty issues. Better brains than yours have pondered these issues. You are paid to fight and to die, and you have successfully done half of that today. Farewell, Captain," Knox waved Schofield away. "Specialist Gordon and Captain Broyles will escort you and your men out."

As he said this, Knox threw Flash Gordon and the

Buck a look—unseen by Schofield—that said: *they are not to leave this place alive.*

Gordon nodded. So did the Buck.

The Delta team swooped in on Schofield's five men, surrounding them perhaps a little more tightly than they needed to. Gordon indicated the door. "Captain . . . if you will."

Schofield entered the elevator shaft, followed by his team.

THROUGHOUT ALL this, the apes sat silently, swaying slightly from side to side, as if their lust for blood was being suppressed only by the chips in their heads.

Schofield stepped out into the elevator shaft, stood at its base, where he saw the huge circular safe-like door set into the wall. He headed for the ladder—

—when suddenly his Delta escorts released the safeties on their guns and aimed them at him and his Marines.

"Hold it right there, Scarecrow," Gordon said.

"Oh, you *cocksuckers* . . ." Mother said.

"Buck?" Bigfoot asked in surprise.

"Buck, how can you do this?" Sanchez said, too, turning to his former commander.

Buck Broyles just shrugged. "Sorry, boys. But you aren't my responsibility anymore."

"You son of a bitch . . ." Sanchez breathed.

During this exchange between the men, Schofield assessed his options and quickly found that there was nothing available. This time they were well and truly screwed.

But then as he gazed at his ring of captors, he noticed that every single one of them wore a silver disc clipped to his lapel.

The silver discs, Schofield thought. *That was it . . .*

And suddenly things began to make sense.

That was how you stayed safe from the apes. If you wore a silver disc, the apes couldn't attack you. The discs were somehow connected to the microchips in the apes' heads, probably by some kind of digital radio signal—

A digital radio signal. Schofield sighed inwardly. Like the binary beep signal Mother had picked up earlier. That was how the Buck had been remotely commanding the apes: with digital signals sent directly to the chips in their brains.

The silver discs probably worked the same way— which was how Pennebaker had been able to enter the fray before to give Schofield information without having to fear the apes.

"Mother," Schofield whispered as he raised his hands above his head. "Still got your AXS-9 there?"

"Yeah?"

"Jam radios, all channels, *now.*"

Mother was also in the process of raising her hands—when suddenly she snapped her right hand down and hit a switch on the AXS-9 spectrum analyzer on her webbing, the switch marked: SIGNAL JAM: ALL CH.

The Delta man beside her swung his gun around, but he never fired.

Because right then another *very loud* sound seized his attention.

The sound of the apes awakening.

The effect of what Mother had done was invisible, but if one could have *seen* the radio spectrum it would have looked like this: a radiating wave of energy had fanned out from Mother's jamming pack, moving outward from her in a circular motion, like expanding ripples in a pond, hitting every wave-emitting device in the area, and turning each device's signal into garbled static.

The result: the silver discs on the ID badges of Knox, the DARPA scientists, the Buck and the Delta team all *instantly became useless.*

From his position in the elevator shaft, Schofield saw what happened next in a kind of hyper-real slow motion.

He saw Knox in the ammo chamber with the army of deadly apes looming above him; saw the three apes nearest to Knox suddenly leap down at him, jaws bared, arms extended, slamming into him, throwing him to the ground, where they fired into him with their M-4s at point-blank range.

In the face of their gunfire, Dr. Malcolm Knox was turned into a bloody mess, his body exploding in a million bullet holes. Grotesquely, the apes kept firing into him long after he was dead.

Complete pandemonium followed . . .

. . . as the rest of the ape army leapt down from the mountain of crates looking for blood.

Different people reacted in different ways.

The DARPA scientists in the chamber spun, eyes wide with horror.

In the elevator shaft, the Delta team also turned, shocked, Gordon and the Buck among them.

Schofield, however, was already moving, calling, "Marines, two hands! Now!"

As for the apes, well, they went apeshit.

Freed from the grip of the silver discs, they launched themselves at the DARPA scientists in the ammo chamber, crashtackling them to the floor, club bing them with the butts of their guns, tearing them apart—as if all their lives they had been waiting to attack their makers.

Screams and cries rang out.

Zak Pennebaker ran for the door to the elevator shaft, crying, "Buck! Do something!" before he himself was crashtackled from behind and assailed by six, then eight, then twelve apes.

He disappeared under their bodies, arms flailing,

screaming in terror, before he was completely over-whelmed by the hairy black monsters.

In the elevator shaft, Flash Gordon and his team of Delta scumbags were caught totally by surprise.

Gordon whirled back to face Schofield, bringing his pistol back around—

—only to see both of Schofield's Desert Eagle pistols aimed directly at his own nose.

"Surprise," Schofield said.

Blam!

Schofield fired.

The apes were now rushing for the door, all three hundred of them, angry and deadly, heading for the elevator shaft.

While they did so, Schofield's Marines did battle with the Delta force surrounding them.

It was a short battle.

For Schofield's men had obeyed Schofield's shouted order—"Marines, two hands!"—so that by now they all held guns in *both* their hands: an MP-7 in one and a pistol in the other.

The five Marines whipped up two guns each—and suddenly they'd evened the odds against the ten-man Delta squad encircling them.

The Marines fired as one, spraying bullets outward, dropping the distracted Delta squad around them.

Six of the Delta men were killed instantly by head shots. The other four went down, wounded but not killed.

The only bad guy left standing was the Buck, mouth open, gun held limply at his side, frozen in shock at the unfolding mayhem around him: the apes were completely out of control; Knox and his scientists were dead; and Schofield's men had just nailed their Delta captors.

A call from Schofield roused him.

"Marines! Up the ladder! Now!"

As his Marines climbed skyward, Schofield grabbed the ladder last of all, shoving past the immobile Buck.

After he was ten feet up, Schofield aimed his pistol at a lever on the big round safe-like door set into the wall of the elevator shaft.

"History lesson for you, Buck," Schofield said. "Happy swimming."

Blam.

Schofield fired, hitting the lever with a spray of sparks.

And at which point all hell really broke loose.

The lever snapped downward, into the RELEASE position.

And the big ten-foot-wide circular door was instantly *flung* open, swinging inward with incredible force, force that came from the weight of ocean water that had been pressing against it from the other side.

This door was one of the floodgates that the Japanese had used in 1943 to flood the tunnels of Hell Island. A door that backed onto the Pacific Ocean itself.

A shocking blast of seawater came rushing in through the circular doorway, slamming into the Buck, lifting him off his feet and hurling him like a rag doll against the opposite wall of the elevator shaft, the force so strong that his skull *cracked* when it hit the concrete.

The roar of the ocean flooding into the elevator shaft was absolutely deafening. It looked like the spray from a giant fireman's hose, a *ten-foot-wide* spray of super-powerful inrushing water.

And one more thing.

The layout of the subterranean ammunition chamber meant that the incoming water flooded *into Chamber No. 2,* where the three hundred apes now stood, trapped.

The apes scrambled across the chamber, wading waist-deep against the powerful waves of whitewater pouring into it.

The water level rose fast—the apes continued howling, struggling against it—but it only took a few seconds for it to hit the upper frame of the doorway to the chamber, sealing off the chamber completely, cutting off the sounds of the three hundred madly-scrambling apes.

And while they could swim short distances, the apes could not swim *underwater.*

They couldn't get out.

Ammunition Chamber No. 2 of Hell Island would be their tomb—three hundred apes, innocent creatures turned into killing machines, would drown in it.

FOUR GORILLAS, however, *did* make it out of the hall before the water completely covered the doorway.

They got to the elevator shaft and started climbing the ladder, heading up and away from the swirling body of ocean water pouring into the concrete shaft beneath them.

Higher up the same ladder, Schofield and his team scaled the shaft as quickly as they could.

The roar of inrushing water drowned out all sound for almost thirty seconds until—ominously—the whole shaft suddenly fell silent.

It wasn't that the water had stopped rushing in: it was just that the water *level* had risen above the floodgate. The ocean was still invading the shaft, just from below its own waterline.

"Keep climbing!" Schofield called up to the others, moving last of all. "We have to get above sea level!"

He looked behind him, saw the four pursuing apes.

Fact: gorillas are much better climbers than human beings.

Schofield yelled, "Guys! We've got company!"

Three-quarters of the way up the shaft was a large horizontal metal grate that folded down across the width of the shaft—notches in its edges allowed it to close around the elevator cables. When closed horizontally, it would completely span the shaft, sealing it off. It was one of the gates the Japanese had created to trap intruders down below.

Schofield saw it. "Mother! When you get to that grate, close it behind you!"

The Marines came to the grate, climbed up past it one at a time—Astro, then Bigfoot, then Sanchez and Mother.

With a loud clang, Sanchez quickly closed one half of the grate. Mother grabbed the other half, just as Schofield reached it . . .

. . . at the same time as a big hairy hand grabbed his ankle and yanked hard!

Schofield slipped down six rungs, clutching with his hands, dropping six feet below the grate, an ape hanging from his left foot.

"Scarecrow!" Mother shouted.

"Close the grate!" Schofield called.

Immediately below him, the ocean water was now *charging* up the vertical elevator shaft. It must have completely filled the ammo chamber—so that now it was racing up the only space left for it to go: the much narrower elevator shaft.

"No!" Mother yelled. To shut the grate was to drown Schofield himself.

"You have to!" Schofield shouted back. "You have to shut them in!"

Schofield glanced downward at the enraged gorilla clutching his left foot. The other three apes were clambering up the ladder close behind it.

He leveled his pistol at the gorilla holding him—

Click.

Dry.

"Shit."

Then suddenly he saw movement out of the corner of his eye and turned to find someone hovering next to his face, level with his head, someone hanging upside-down!

Mother.

Hanging fully stretched, inverted, her legs held by Sanchez and Bigfoot up at the grate, herself holding pistols in both hands.

"No heroic sacrifices today, buddy," she said to Schofield.

She then opened fire with both her guns, blasting the ape holding him to pieces. The ape released him, Mother chucked her guns, grabbed Schofield by his webbing and suddenly, *whoosh,* both Mother *and* Schofield were lifted up the shaft by Sanchez and Bigfoot, up past the half-closed grate, where once they were up, Astro slammed down the other half and snapped shut its lock.

The three remaining apes and the rising water hit the grate moments later, the water pinning the screaming apes to the underside of the grate until it rose past them, swallowing them, climbing a further ten feet up the shaft, before it abruptly stopped, having come level with the sea outside, now forbidden by physics from rising any further.

Schofield's Marines gazed down at the sloshing body of water from their ladder above, breathless and exhausted, but safe, and now the only creatures—man or ape—still breathing on Hell Island.

FOUR HOURS later, a lone plane arrived on the landing strip of Hell Island. It was a gigantic Air Force C-17A Globemaster, one of the biggest cargo-lifters in the world, capable of holding over two hundred armed personnel, or perhaps three hundred sedated apes.

Its six-man crew were a little surprised to find only five United States Marines—dirty, bloody and battle-weary—waiting on the tarmac to greet them.

Its co-pilot came out and met Schofield, shouted above the whine of the plane's enormous jet engines: "Who the hell are you? We're here to pick up a bunch of DARPA guys, Delta specialists, and some mysterious cargo that we're not allowed to look at. Nobody said anything about Marines."

Schofield just shook his head.

"There's no cargo," he said. "Not anymore. Now, if you don't mind, would you please take us home."

Coming in January 2011 from Pocket Books

Matthew Reilly's

THE FIVE GREATEST WARRIORS

The *New York Times* bestseller and sequel to

SEVEN DEADLY WONDERS

and

THE SIX SACRED STONES

Turn the page for an exciting preview!

THE SECOND VERTEX
BENEATH THE CAPE OF GOOD HOPE
SOUTH AFRICA
DECEMBER 17, 2007, 0325 HOURS

J ACK WEST fell.

Fast.

Down into the black abyss beneath the inverted pyramid that was the Second Vertex.

As he plummeted into the darkness, Jack looked up to see the gigantic pyramid receding into the distance, getting smaller and smaller, the jagged walls of the abyss crowding in around it.

Falling through the air beside him was Switchblade, the Japanese-American US Marine who moments earlier had betrayed Wolf and almost derailed his plan to insert the Second Pillar in its rightful place at the peak of the pyramid. It turned out that Switchblade's Japanese blood was more important to him than his American upbringing.

But after a last-ditch swing from Jack and a desperate struggle above the abyss, Jack had jammed the Pillar in place just as the two of them had dropped from the upside-down peak and commenced their fall into the bottomless darkness.

The rocky walls of the abyss rushed past Jack in a blur of speed. He fell with Switchblade in a tumbling ungainly way, their limbs still awkwardly entwined. As they plummeted, Switchblade punched and scratched and lashed out at Jack, before grabbing his shirt and glaring at him with baleful eyes, screaming above the wind, "You! You did this! At least I know you'll die with me!"

Jack parried away the crazed Marine's blows as they fell.

"No, I won't . . ." he said grimly as he suddenly kicked Switchblade square in the chest, pushing himself away from the suicidal Marine—at the same time, grabbing something from a holster on Switchblade's back, something that every Force Recon Marine carried.

His Maghook.

Switchblade saw the device in Jack's hands, and his eyes widened in horror. He tried to grab it, but now Jack was out of his reach.

"No! No!!"

Still falling, Jack pivoted in the air, turning his back on Switchblade to face the wall of the abyss.

He fired the Maghook.

Whump!

The high-tech grappling hook flew out from its

gunlike launcher, its metal claws snapping outward as it did so, its 150-foot-long reinforced-nylon cable wobbling like a tail behind it.

The grappling hook's claws hit the wall of the abyss, scraped against it, searching for a purchase before—whack!—they found an uneven section of rock and caught—and instantly Jack's cable went taut—and his fall was abruptly and violently arrested, and it took all his might to keep a grip on the Maghook's launcher.

Jack swung into the wall of the abyss with a colossal thump that almost dislocated his left shoulder.

Silence.

For a moment, Jack hung there from the cable of Switchblade's Maghook, dangling from the rocky vertical wall of the great abyss, high above the center of the world and at least a thousand feet below the upside-down bronze pyramid of the Vertex. Despite its immense size, it now looked positively tiny.

Closing his eyes, Jack exhaled the biggest sigh of relief of his life.

"What the hell were you thinking, Jack?" he whispered to himself, catching his breath, letting the adrenaline rush subside.

A flutter of feathers made him spin, and suddenly a small brown peregrine falcon alighted on his shoulder.

Horus.

His faithful bird pecked affectionately at his ear.

Jack smiled wearily but genuinely. "Thanks, bird. I'm glad I survived, too."

Distant shouts from up in the Vertex made him look up—Wolf's people must have noticed that the Pillar had been set in place and were now sending men to get it.

Jack sighed. He could never hope to climb back up in time to catch them, let alone stop them. He might have saved the world and their lives and killed the traitor in their midst, but now the bad guys were going to get the booty: the Second Pillar's reward, the mysterious concept known only as heat.

But there was nothing Jack could do about that now.

He turned to Horus. "You coming?"

And with that, he gazed up at the pyramid high above him and after a deep breath, reeled in the Maghook, grabbed a handhold on the rough surface of the abyss's wall, and began the long climb upward.

It took Jack nearly an hour to scale the wall of the abyss—by firing the Maghook up it, then ascending its cable 150 feet at a time.

It was slow going, since the rocky wall was largely sheer and slick, and sometimes the grappling hook found no purchase at all and just fell back down toward Jack.

But after about fifty minutes of such climbing, Jack

slid over the edge of a stone rail and lay on his back on the precipice, his chest heaving, sucking in air. Horus landed lightly beside him.

When Jack sat up, he saw the magnificent underground city constructed in supplication to the inverted pyramid, with its hollow towers, its streets of inky black liquid and, through the forest of bridges and towers, the massive ziggurat rising in its center; the whole scene lit by Wolf's dying amber flares.

Of course, the entire supercavern was now deserted, Wolf's force having long since departed.

Also gone, Jack noted sadly, were his companions, the Adamson twins and the Sea Ranger. Jack imagined that, thinking him dead, they had rightly hurried back down the long underwater passageway that led back to the open ocean in the Sea Ranger's submarine—

Movement.

Jack spun, his eyes focusing on the summit of the ziggurat, just visible between all the towers.

"Oh my God . . ." he breathed, registering who it was.

There, sitting totally alone on top of the mighty ziggurat, his head bowed, one of his arms in a sling, was a small boy, his daughter's best friend, Alby Calvin.

Left alone in this enormous space, with his wounded shoulder aching and with Jack West Jr.'s battered FDNY fireman's helmet sitting in his lap, Alby had given up all hope of escape and was waiting for the last flares to fizzle out, when he heard the shouting voice.

"Alby! Albeeee!"

He snapped to look up—fresh tears still running down his cheeks—to see a tiny figure over by the edge of the abyss waving his arms.

Jack.

Alby's eyes nearly popped out of his head.

Jack negotiated his way across the underground mini-metropolis, over to the central ziggurat, using Wolf's plank bridges where he could and swinging across the wider thoroughfares with the Maghook where he had to.

The black ooze that filled the city's streets appeared to be a thick mudlike substance—semiliquid and goopy. If you fell into it, you didn't get out.

As he traversed the avenues, he tried his radio. "Sea Ranger, come in? Do you read me?"

No reply.

His small handheld radio didn't have the signal strength to reach the Sea Ranger in his submarine.

Moving in his unorthodox way, Jack hurried across the underground city.

At last, he came to the base of the ziggurat and bounded up its stairs, arriving at the roof, where he slid to Alby's side and embraced him as if he were his own son.

Likewise, Alby hurled his good arm around Jack, closing his eyes, tears streaming down his cheeks.

"I thought I was going to die here, by myself in the dark . . ." he whimpered.

"I wouldn't let that happen, Alby." Jack released the boy from his bear hug. "You're too good a friend to Lily . . . and to me. Plus, your mother would absolutely kill me."

Alby stared at him. "You just fell into a chasm with a guy who was trying to kill everyone in the whole world and you're afraid of my mom?"

"Hell yeah. When it comes to your well-being, your mom's scary."

Alby smiled at that. Then he lifted Jack's fireman's helmet from his lap and offered it to Jack. "I think this belongs to you."

Jack took it and placed it on his head, pulling the chin strap tight. Just putting it on made him look and feel whole again. "Thanks. I've been missing that."

He nodded at Alby's sling. "So what happened to you?"

"I got shot."

"Jesus Christ, your mom's really gonna kill me. By who?"

"By that guy who fell into the chasm with you. Back in Africa, in the Neetha kingdom."

"Maybe there is justice in the world," Jack said. "Come on, little buddy, this ain't over yet, we gotta move. We have to catch up with the Sea Ranger and the twins."

He hefted Alby to his feet.

"How are we going to do that?" Alby asked.

"The old-fashioned way," Jack said.

Jack and Alby hustled back across the city, heading for the northeast harbor, racing over bridges or swinging—with Alby piggybacking on Jack's back.

After twenty minutes of this kind of travel, they came to the hill of stone steps that descended into the enclosed harbor there.

"I just hope they haven't cleared the tunnel and got to the open sea yet," Jack said, pulling off his helmet and stepping knee deep into the water.

Then he began banging the metal helmet against the first stone step beneath the waterline.

Dull clangs rang out. Three short ones, three long ones, then three short ones again.

Morse code, Alby realized.

Jack clanged the helmet against the stone some more, punching out another code.

"Let's hope the sonar operator knows his Morse," he said.

"How will they know it's you?" Alby said. "They might think it's a trap, that it's Wolf trying to bring them back."

"I'm signaling: 'S.O.S. COWBOYS COME BACK.'

The twins only just got their nicknames, nicknames Wolf can't possibly know."

"How will you know if they've heard you?"

Jack sat down on the top step, holding his helmet limply in his hand. "I can't know. All we can do now is wait and hope they haven't already gone out of range."

Jack and Alby waited, sitting on the top step of the hill of stairs rising out of the ancient walled harbor, in the dying yellow light of Wolf's flares.

The shadows lengthened as the flares began to sink and fizzle out. The majestic underground city and the pyramid lording over it, having existed in darkness for so many centuries, were about to be plunged back into blackness.

And as the last flare began to flicker and die, Jack put his arm around Alby. "I'm sorry, kid."

The flare went out.

Darkness engulfed them.

A moment later, a colossal whooshing noise filled the air, followed by splashing and the sound of water running off the flanks of a—

Bam!

A spotlight lanced out of the darkness, exposing Jack and Alby on their step, illuminating them in a circle of harsh white light. They had to shield their eyes, the light was so bright.

A Russian-made *Kilo*-class submarine loomed in the water in front of them, dark and immense.

A hatch opened beside the external spotlight and out of it stepped J. J. Wickham, the Sea Ranger, Jack's longtime friend and captain of the *Indian Raider*. With him were the Adamson twins, Lachlan and Julius, Jack's mathematical and historical experts.

"Jack!" the Sea Ranger said. "And you must be Alby—Jack's told me all about you. Well, come on! Get in! We were in the middle of a perfectly good escape when you called us back. You can tell us all about how you escaped certain death when we're out of here. Now, move!"

Jack could only smile. He grabbed Alby's hand and they leaped down into the water and clambered aboard the submarine.

An hour later, the sub emerged from the ancient tunnel and powered out into the Indian Ocean, barely beating a South African Navy frigate sent to investigate the waters off the Cape of Good Hope.

Once they were safe and clear, the Sea Ranger sought Jack out in his quarters. He found him sitting with Alby, re-dressing the little boy's bullet wound.

"You're lucky the bullet went right through," Jack was saying. "Took a little chunk of your shoulder with it. You'll have full range of motion again in about six weeks."

"What'll I tell my mom?" Alby asked.

Jack whispered conspiratorially, "I was kinda hoping you'd let me put a cast on your arm and we'd tell your mum you broke your arm falling out of a tree."

"Done."

"Er, Jack," Wickham interrupted. "What do we do now?"

Jack looked up.

"We regroup. As soon as we're in safe radio space, call the others on the *Halicarnassus* and tell them to rendezvous with us at World's End."

"World's End? I thought it'd been abandoned."

"It *was* abandoned, which is why it's perfect for us right now. Zoe and Wizard know the coordinates."

"I'll get on it." Wickham left.

Jack watched him go, lost in thought.

Alby was eyeing Jack. "Mr. West?"

"Yeah?" Jack came out of his reverie.

"That Wolf guy has the first two Pillars, fully charged, plus the Firestone and the Philosopher's Stone. That English lady, Iolanthe, has the Fourth Pillar. We have no sacred stones, no Pillars, no nothing. Have we lost this fight?"

Jack looked down at his feet. Then he replied, "Alby, we're playing a different game to them: they want power and strength and riches. We just want to keep the world turning. And while we're still breathing, we're still in the game. No fight is over till the last punch is thrown."

CAPE TOWN, SOUTH AFRICA
DECEMBER 17, 2007, 0600 HOURS

The South African Navy patrol boat came alongside a military dock in the shadow of Table Mountain.

As soon as its gangway hit the dock, Jack West Sr.—Jack's father and bitter rival in this quest—strode off the boat and stepped straight into a waiting limousine. Known as Wolf, in his late fifties, he was burly and strong, and he looked just like Jack West Jr., with a creased face and ice blue eyes, only twenty years older.

With Wolf was his five-person entourage, a mixed group that represented the coalition of nations and organizations backing Wolf's participation in the quest to lay the Six Pillars at the Six Vertices: China, Saudi Arabia, the Royal Families of Europe, and his own American military-industrial cabal, the Caldwell Group.

Representing China was Colonel Mao Gongli. Known as the Butcher of Tiananmen, he'd supplied Chinese weapons and manpower to the cause. His dead eyes hardly ever registered emotion, not even when he shot someone in the back of the head.

Representing the Caldwell Group along with Wolf was Wolf's second son, a cold-blooded CIEF operator, formerly of Delta, who went by the call sign Rapier.

Representing Saudi Arabia was the man who

had betrayed Jack West's team earlier in the mission: thin and skeletal, with a long ratlike nose, he was an agent of the notorious Saudi Royal Intelligence Service known as Vulture.

Accompanying Vulture was a handsome young captain from the United Arab Emirates named Scimitar. The first son of its chief sheik—and thus the older brother of Pooh Bear—Scimitar had joined Vulture in his betrayal of Jack and Pooh Bear, even going so far as to leave his younger brother to die in an Ethiopian mine.

The last member of Wolf's entourage was a woman, a beautiful and poised young lady in her thirties: Ms. Iolanthe Compton-Jones, the Keeper of the Royal Records of the House of Windsor.

As the six of them sat in the limousine bound for Cape Town's military airstrip, Wolf pulled a glittering Pillar from his pack and handed it to Vulture.

"As per our bargain, Saudi," Wolf said. "Once I got the Second Pillar, fully charged, you became entitled to the First, also charged."

Vulture took the First Pillar, charged at the First Vertex at Abu Simbel, eyeing it with barely concealed delight.

When he replied, his eyes scanned Wolf's closely. "That was indeed our bargain, Colonel West. I thank you for honoring the agreement. I wish you good fortune in the remainder of your mission. Should you require any further assistance from the Kingdom of Saudi Arabia, you need only call."

The limousine arrived at the military base. Passing the gatehouse without any checks, it arrived at two Gulfstream-IV private jets parked side by side.

Vulture and Scimitar boarded one and immediately departed.

Wolf, Rapier, Mao, and Iolanthe watched them go.

Mao said, "I don't trust the Saudis for a moment. They have money, but they have all the honor of a gang of desert bandits."

"They had their use." Iolanthe shrugged. "We used them."

"And they came through," Wolf said.

"So what now?" Mao asked.

"Now," Wolf said, "we get a reprieve of approximately three months, till March of next year. And we'll need that time to research the locations of the remaining four Pillars and Vertices."

Iolanthe said, "I have the Fourth Pillar already. The Third Pillar is believed to be in the possession of the Japanese Imperial Family. I understand that after the Second World War, a team of American agents was sent to find it but failed. Is this true?"

Wolf nodded. "Hirohito hid it during the war. We never found it. We assume it's still somewhere in Japan.

"Which means we have in our possession the Second and the Fourth Pillars," he continued. "The Third, Fifth, and Sixth Pillars must still be found. Likewise, all four of the remaining Vertices need to be discovered before the return of the Dark Sun in March of next year. I've had my scientific people working on the Stonehenge data while we've been traipsing around Africa, and I imagine our new African friend, the Neetha holy man, will have unique knowledge as well."

"What about this coalition of minnow nations?" Mao growled. "This group led by your first son, the Australian."

"He doesn't lead them anymore," Wolf said, thinking of Jack falling into the abyss. "Without him, they're weakened but not destroyed. The Irish woman is formidable, as we discovered in Africa, and Professor Epper is resilient. In the short term, pressure needs to be exerted on their masters."

"And in the longer term? What if they cross our path again?"

"Then we crush them with overwhelming force," Wolf said.

"Good," Mao said. "Finally."

AIRSPACE OVER NAMIBIA
DECEMBER 17, 2007, 0645 HOURS

The *Halicarnassus* thundered through the sky, banking dramatically to evade the line of glowing tracer rounds that sizzled through the air all around it, tracers that had been unleashed by a pursuing South African Air Force F-15, the first of four fighters chasing it.

The big black 747 rocketed westward, crossing the boundary between the drab brown Namib Desert and the Atlantic Ocean, heading out over the vast expanse of blue.

It had been fleeing like this for almost an hour, since South Africa—all their expenses paid by the Saudis—had scrambled an air patrol to take them out: and in the last ten minutes, as the fighters had caught up with them, it had become a running aerial gun battle.

As the *Halicarnassus* flew, it returned fire at the lead F-15 from one of the 50mm gun turrets mounted on the inner sections of its wings.

Manning the starboard gun—facing backward as the jumbo screamed forward through the air—was Zoe Kissane. She drew a bead on the trailing F-15 and assailed it with a withering blast of 50mm fire.

But the South African pilot was skilled and he barrel rolled clear of the stream of gunfire.

"Sky Monster . . . !" Zoe called into her radio. "This is like shooting at goddamn bumblebees! What's our plan!"

Sky Monster's voice came in from the cockpit: "They might be smaller and faster than we are, but we can fly farther than they can. They gotta be running low on fuel. So the plan is: you keep holding them off while I get us as far as possible over the ocean, till they decide they're too low on gas and have to turn back. We beat them with range."

Sky Monster proved to be correct.

A few minutes later, the lead South African fighter loosed a single AIM-9 Sidewinder air-to-air missile and bugged out, heading back for the mainland with his buddies.

Zoe took care of the Sidewinder with a directed microwave burst that literally cooked the missile's dome-mounted infrared targeting system, and the missile ditched harmlessly into the ocean.

The aerial battle over, she wearily headed up to the 747's cockpit, where she found Wizard and Lily with Sky Monster.

Oddly, they were grinning, beaming even.

"Zoe," Wizard said, "we just got a call from the Sea Ranger. Jack's alive and he has Alby with him. The Sea Ranger has them both. They want us to rendezvous at World's End."

Zoe sighed with relief. "Thank God. Take us there."

LITTLE MCDONALD ISLAND
INDIAN OCEAN
DECEMBER 20, 2007
3 DAYS LATER

At the bottom of the Indian Ocean, in one of the most remote regions of the world, there can be found a cluster of barren rocky islands.

The Kerguélen Islands are administered by France, while the Prince Edward Islands are claimed by South Africa. But south of them all, battered year-round by icy Antarctic winds and the rolling waves of the southern seas, is the Heard group of islands. They are administered by Australia.

One of the Heard islands is Little McDonald Island. It has no wildlife and little flora. There is literally no reason to go there. Which is probably why it was used during World War II as a resupply base for the Australian Navy, complete with fuel dumps, storage warehouses, and even a short landing strip.

By the 1990s, its use as a base was long obsolete and it was shut down in late 1991. Whole containers of canned food and diesel fuel had been left there, and in sixteen years, not a single can had been stolen. It wasn't worth the effort to get there.

Which was why no one in the world noticed the Kilo-class submarine and the black Boeing 747 that arrived at Little McDonald Island two days after the high drama at the Second Vertex.

Of course, they knew the island by another name: World's End.

The reunion of Jack and the team was a joyous occasion.

Lily leaped into Jack's arms, hugged him tightly—then she ran over to Alby and hugged him even harder.

Zoe and Jack also embraced warmly, holding each other for a full minute.

"Alby told me all about what happened with the Neetha," Jack said softly. "You must have been incredible."

Zoe didn't answer.

She just began sobbing on Jack's shoulder, burying her head in his neck, unleashing the pent-up stress and emotion that had been inside her since her bloody encounter with the lost tribe of African cannibals.

When at last she spoke, she said in a hoarse voice, "Next time, let's let somebody else save the world."

Jack laughed, stroking her hair gently.

As he held Zoe, he saw Wizard and, with him, the archaeologist and Neetha expert, Diane Cassidy, plus the Neetha youth, Ono, who had helped them during their escape from the remote tribe.

Wizard smiled. "Clearly, it's not the fall that kills you, Jack."

"Right," Jack said.

"Hey," Lily said, looking around, suddenly alarmed. "Where's Pooh Bear? And where's Stretch?"

Once the reunion was complete and introductions made, the team went inside a decrepit old warehouse beside the island's airstrip. Water was heated for showers; canned food was opened and eaten; and Jack explained to the others what had happened to him before he'd arrived at Cape Town.

He told them what had happened at the mine in Ethiopia, including the betrayal of Vulture and Scimitar, his own gruesome crucifixion, his and Pooh Bear's bloody escape and the parting gift they'd received from the Ethiopian slave force there: the fabled Twin Tablets of Thuthmosis.

Jack pulled the two stone tablets from his backpack, which had been kept on the submarine during the events at the Second Vertex.

Wizard audibly gasped at the sight of them.

"If Thuthmosis was actually Moses," he said, "then that would make these the Ten Com—"

"Yes," Jack said.

"Goodness-gracious-Mother-of . . ."

"As for Stretch," Jack went on, "Wolf didn't bring him to the mine. Instead, he took him back to the Mossad in Israel, to claim the sixteen-million-dollar bounty on Stretch's head."

"Oh no . . ." Lily breathed.

Jack said, "After Pooh Bear and I escaped from that mine in Ethiopia, we headed south to the old farm in Kenya. But when I set out for Zanzibar to find the Sea Ranger, Pooh Bear didn't come with me. He went off to rescue Stretch from the Mossad's dungeons. That was nine days ago. I haven't heard from him since."

A solemn silence descended on the group.

Lily broke it.

"When we were in the Hanging Gardens," she said, "Stretch defied an Israeli Army squad and saved my life. He chose us over them and now they're making him pay."

She recalled the scene vividly: trapped in a filling pool of quicksand, she had stood on Stretch's shoulders to poke her nose and mouth above the surface, while he had breathed through his sniper rifle's gun barrel, using it as a snorkel.

Alby asked, "What does the Mossad do to Israeli soldiers who switch sides and fight against them?"

Jack threw a glance at Zoe and Wizard. Zoe nodded silently. Wizard just bowed his head.

When he finally answered, Jack spoke in a low voice, his face serious. "The Mossad isn't known for showing mercy to its enemies. Traitors like Stretch receive the harshest punishment of all. There are stories of high-security desert prisons, their locations kept strictly secret, where high-grade prisoners are kept under twenty-four-hour guard and . . . mistreated . . . for years."

"Mistreated?" Lily said.

"For *years*?" Alby said.

Jack said, "If Pooh Bear even manages to discover where they're keeping Stretch, getting in and busting him out will be an all-but-impossible task. It'd be like breaking into Guantanamo Bay and running off with a terrorist."

Lily said, "You did that once, Daddy. Can't we go and help Pooh Bear?"

Jack looked at her sadly. "Lily. Honey. There are some operations that even I wouldn't dare attempt, and this is one of them. I'm sorry, I really am, but we have to leave that to Pooh Bear and keep our eyes on the larger mission. It's a hard decision for me to make, really hard, believe me, but weighing up the possibilities and probabilities of success, I have to make it this way. I'm sorry."

Jack bowed his head, but not before he saw the look Lily gave him—a look he'd never seen on her face before. It was a look of the most profound disappointment, and at that moment, he hated himself.

"So what *are* we going to do now then?" Lily asked in a sour tone.

"First of all," Jack said, "Alby is going back to his mother in Perth; she'll be beside herself when she sees his arm. And after Christmas, I'll be sending you to join him. Keep you two out of harm's way for a while."

"*What!*" Lily protested. "What about the rest of you?"

"We're going to try to find the remaining Pillars and Vertices before the world ends in March of next year."

Don't miss

THE FIVE GREATEST WARRIORS

Coming in January from Pocket Books!